D0456208

Sun Kissed

CALGARY PUBLIC LIBRARY

APR   2016

Sun Kissed

An Orchid Island Novel

JoAnn Ross

Copyright © 2015 by Castlelough Publishing, LLC
Cover design by Syd Gill Designs

Publisher's note: This is a work of fiction. The characters in this book have no existence outside the imagination of the author and have no relation to anyone bearing the same name or names. All incidents are pure invention and any resemblance to actual persons, events, or locales is entirely coincidental.

ISBN-10: 1941134130
ISBN-13: 9781941134139

From *New York Times* bestselling author JoAnn Ross comes the first in a new series set in paradise. From its soaring mountain peaks to its turquoise lagoons, Orchid Island, the jewel of the Pacific, offers endless opportunities for romance to bloom.

Lani Breslin has had it with the mainland rat race. A free spirit in an eccentric family, she's returned to her Orchid Island home to live an idyllic life. And if her brother happens to send along a yummy hunk to seduce her? That's just fine with Lani.

Police detective Donovan Quinn's last case nearly killed him. Burned out and still recuperating from an injury, he escapes to the tranquility of Orchid Island to reboot his life. It's a sweet surprise to discover Lani has blossomed like one of the island's tropical flowers, even if the Bro Code says you shouldn't crave moonlit kisses from your best friend's sister.

As Donovan struggles to resist Lani's charms, matters get more complicated when her best friend's fiancé goes missing and he finds himself caught up in a chase involving the FBI, sunken treasure, and pirates. It's not easy solving a mystery when he keeps stumbling over his heart and may have to choose between the opportunity of a lifetime or a lifetime in paradise with the woman he loves.

1

Portland Police Bureau Detective Donovan Quinn was not filled with what the residents of the neighboring Hawai'ian Islands would call the aloha spirit. He was hot, thirsty, tired, and cursing his decision to come to Orchid Island. Back in Oregon, the idea had made sense—a remote, tranquil place to escape the demons that had been haunting him. And worse yet, the sense of drifting, almost like those people who claimed to have near-death experiences, floating above their bodies, watching their lives and souls drift away.

He'd talked with the department chaplain. With the shrink who'd offered to prescribe anti-depressants, which he wasn't yet prepared to take. He'd also gone out to dinner with his best friends, only to belatedly discover that they'd planned an intervention.

"You've been there," Nate Breslin had reminded him over fried clam strips and shrimp po'boys with him and Tess Lombardi at Bon Temps on the coast in Shelter Bay. "It's a tropical paradise. Lush greenery, palm trees, sparkling beaches, turquoise waters, and the most beautiful women found anywhere on earth."

The horror novelist had turned toward his fiancée and given her a quick kiss. "Present company excluded, of course."

"Thank you, darling." Her smile suggested that he'd be rewarded for that qualification once they got home to Sunset Point.

Then she'd turned back to Donovan, her expression turning serious. "When Nate took me to the island to meet his family, I was tempted to stay. And I swear, within the first few hours of landing, I was more relaxed than I've ever been in my life."

Given that the Multnomah County deputy district attorney had recently escaped a harrowing ordeal that had nearly cost Tess her life, that had been saying something.

"You'd probably be out of work," he'd countered. Especially given her workaholic habits. Though he had noticed that she'd actually begun taking time for a personal life since falling for Nate. Even more so since returning from their Thanksgiving trip to the Pacific island. "Given that there's undoubtedly even less crime on Orchid Island than here in Shelter Bay."

"That would probably be true." She'd snagged a clam strip from her fiancé's plate and dipped it into the restaurant's signature *comeback* sauce. "But I was seriously tempted. And if you're not going to go there for yourself, Donovan, please do it for me." She'd reached across the table and put a hand on his. "Bad enough that you landed in the hospital because of me; you've recently been through a horrible personal experience. If you're not going to stick with therapy, try the meds, or cancel that damn speech you agreed to give in Hawai'i, the least you can do is steal some additional time for R and R."

"I can't cancel the speech, because I gave my word." Which had been nine months ago. Before his life had begun unraveling at the seams.

So, he was going to give the speech. But, as Tess had known he would, he'd caved in on taking a side trip to Nate's home island.

He should have taken the three-hour flight delay before departure from PDX as a sign. The delay had him arriving in Honolulu with minutes to spare before giving a speech on Pacific Northwest serial killer clusters at a joint O'ahu Police Department and FBI conference. The speech had been booked by the special agent in charge of the Portland FBI field office, who'd been actively recruiting him for the past year.

It would not only polish his credentials for the lengthy acceptance procedure, Donovan had been told, but hanging out with some agents in a social situation would allow him to get a feel for the type of men and women he could be working with.

His speech, centered on possible reasons for the high body count in an area of the country FBI profiler John Douglas had once referred to as "America's killing fields," had been well received. The Cascades Killer had terrorized the mountainous region from southern Oregon up to the Canadian border for nearly a decade. After inheriting the case when the original detective retired, Donovan had upped his professional profile by apprehending the serial killer by using methods he'd learned from the FBI Behavioral Research and Instruction Unit.

While all serial killers were heinous, this one had been particularly so, targeting entire families camping in the Cascade Mountains. Last month, his partner, a divorced father of three who hadn't been able to overcome the nightmares of all those other murdered children, had committed suicide, leaving Donovan with what both his shrink and police chaplain had diagnosed as survivor guilt.

Putting a name to his problem hadn't done much to help, and while talking about those crimes as he'd forced his way through the speech, he'd wondered how many of the conference attendees in the standing-room-only audience were concealing the same problem. Afterwards, feeling the walls closing in on him, Donovan had passed on the special agents' invitation to have drinks in the bar, reluctantly agreeing to a rain check when he returned to Honolulu on his way back to the mainland.

Now, sixteen hours into an already over-long day, as his shoes filled with sand and he melted under the tropical sun, Donovan had come to the conclusion his mistake had been buying into Nate's sales pitch that palm trees, sparkling beaches, turquoise waters, and stunning women were exactly what he needed to regain his mojo.

So far—except for the aerial view of lush green mountains from the commuter flight to the island of Kaua'i, where he'd boarded a ferry for the thirty-minute ride to Orchid Island— the only foliage Donovan had seen was the tall, tasseled sugarcane flanking the road the taxi driver had turned onto soon after leaving the ferry terminal.

After what seemed an eternity of tearing along in a cloud of red dust, with the man apparently determined to hit every pothole in the dirt road, steam had started rising from beneath the hood of the ancient taxi. While the driver waited for whatever consisted of a motor club on Orchid Island to arrive to repair the radiator, Donovan had begun walking.

That had been twenty long, hot minutes ago, and with his recently injured ankle aching like a son of a bitch, he'd made the decision that if he didn't reach Nate's beach house (which he hadn't owned the first and only time Donovan had been here) within the next thirty seconds, he was going to throw himself, fully clothed, into the Pacific Ocean. Then, once he had cooled off, he was going to trudge back up that damn cane road, flag down the first car he saw, and beg, if necessary, a ride to the ferry terminal, where he could begin the long journey back home to Portland.

It was then that he saw her.

At first, Donovan wondered if the vision might be nothing but a mirage, the product of his heat-crazed mind. She was clad in a brilliantly flowered bikini top and cutoff jeans, her skin tanned to a warm, dark honey, her hair sunlit strands of glistening copper, gold and bronze. If she had been perched on a rock jutting out of the water, instead of sitting atop the roof of the vine-covered house, Donovan could have easily believed that he had stumbled upon a mythical siren. If she wasn't a hallucination, she was definitely a sign that things were looking up.

* * *

LANI BRESLIN RECOGNIZED him immediately. He had, unsurprisingly, grown older, and the frown lines cut between his brows had her wondering if his devastating smile had diminished in wattage. Not that she was at all interested, having gotten her fill of that smile years ago.

At the moment, however, the individual trudging through the sparkling coral sand was definitely not at his charismatic best. He had discarded his gray suit jacket and tie and rolled his starched white sleeves up to the elbow, but his attire was far more suited to Oregon rain than the tropical Orchid Island sun. And his shoes—black wingtips, for heaven's sake, Lani thought critically—were definitely not proper beach footwear. No wonder he was limping.

Since the only two residences on this stretch of isolated beach were her own cottage and this one, Lani put down her hammer with a resigned sigh and waited.

From her vantage point above him, she noticed the almost imperceptible straightening of his spine and the squaring of broad shoulders. He'd come a long, long way in the past fifteen years. Not only was former Portland patrolman Donovan Quinn now a detective, from what her brother had told her, he was the top candidate for chief of the Portland Police Bureau at the same time he was being actively recruited by the FBI.

His ability to slip unconsciously into a public persona of masculine authority was, along with the suit, evidence that he was no longer that reckless young cop she'd met so many years ago. He'd changed. But hadn't they all? Nate's name now appeared on all the bestseller lists, and she certainly wasn't the petulant, self-centered teenage girl she'd been back then.

Still, Lani was somewhat saddened by the idea that Donovan had changed so drastically. All the professional success Nate had told her about hadn't been kind to him. His six-foot, broad-shouldered frame had lost weight to the point of being almost gaunt.

"Hello," he called up to her, dropping his luggage onto the sand. "I'm looking for Nate Breslin's cottage."

Of course he was. Remembering Nate's promise to send her something special for Christmas, Lani vowed to give her older brother a piece of her mind at the very first opportunity.

"You've found it." Her calm voice betrayed none of her annoyance.

"Thank God. I was beginning to feel like Robinson Crusoe."

"This is one of the most deserted stretches of beach on the island," Lani acknowledged. "That's why Nate picked it. He values his privacy." She didn't add that the beach's remoteness held the same appeal for her.

"I know about his penchant for being off the beaten track," Donovan said. "His house on the Oregon Coast is even more remote than this place. You practically need a mountain goat to climb up that road of his...I'm forgetting my manners. I'm Donovan Quinn."

He'd taken off the aviator sunglasses, revealing deep shadows beneath midnight-blue eyes. "Introductions aren't necessary, Donovan. Despite the fact that you seem to have taken to dressing like an undertaker, I had no problem recognizing you."

Donovan shaded his eyes with his hand as he looked up at her. There was something naggingly familiar about the redhead. They'd met before, he determined, but as demanding as his life had been, especially the past few months, what with Tess's stalker, followed by his partner's suicide, Donovan couldn't imagine forgetting this woman.

Although her eyes were hidden by an oversized pair of shades that reminded him of Audrey Hepburn in *Breakfast at Tiffany's*, it was her fiery hair, pulled up into a messy knot atop her head, that rang a distant bell. He forced his mind to concentrate, to remember.

Eventually, a hazy vision stirred. One of a fourteen year old with a mouthful of braces who'd surprised her older brother with a visit one long-ago winter vacation. A teen who'd been less than pleased to discover that she would be sharing that brother with an outspoken rookie cop.

The friendship between the novelist and the patrolman only six weeks out of the police academy had begun purely by chance. Nate had been researching his second novel, and since his protagonist was a Portland patrolman, he had arranged to spend his nights in a cop ride-along program.

After a week of boring, routine calls, they'd gotten involved in a hair-raising adventure. The high-speed chase of an armed robbery suspect, which made every police movie they had ever seen pale by comparison, had ended abruptly at a warehouse by the docks where the suspect took an elderly night watchman hostage.

The standoff had gone on for hours before Donovan was able to convince his superiors that he had learned his way around every inch of this particular warehouse while working on the loading dock to put himself through Portland State.

As dawn had broken on the horizon, his heart beating wildly and his body pumped with adrenaline, he'd crept stealthily through the shadows, ultimately freeing the watchman and apprehending the perpetrator, who'd still managed to put a twenty-two slug in Donovan's shoulder before being handcuffed.

The following week, the rookie cop had been rewarded with a departmental commendation, Nate had enough material for ten books, and the kid sister had returned to Orchid Island in a teenage huff.

No. It couldn't be her.

"Lani?" he asked hesitatingly, still having problems processing the idea that this hot female could be Nate's skinny, redheaded, smart-mouthed kid sister.

"Got it on the first try. Congratulations. I was wondering how long it'd take for you to make the connection."

"How could I forget you?" he hedged, unwilling to admit that he hadn't immediately recognized her. That admission would lead to the less-than-complimentary implication that Lani Breslin had changed dramatically over the past fifteen years.

"How indeed?" she asked with a shake of her head. "Especially after I ruined your holidays."

"You weren't that bad." Okay, that was a lie. She'd been a petulant pain in the ass even as he'd done everything humanly possible to welcome her to Portland.

He'd offered to take her to the zoo on his day off, but she'd professed an allergy to wild animals. The Japanese Gardens were out, as was a Trailblazers' game since she had no interest in basketball. And FYI, according to Nate's sister, *The Nutcracker*, which he'd also suggested, despite having preferred to be zapped with his own Taser than spend a Sunday afternoon at the ballet, was for little kids.

"Besides, it was only natural that you'd resent Nate spending so much time with a stranger after you'd flown all the way across the Pacific to be with him," he said.

"You don't have to be so chivalrous, Donovan," she said, waving away his attempt to excuse her behavior. "I was a brat. I'm surprised you didn't toss me into the river." A smile played at the corners of her full lips. "Especially when I crashed that intimate little New Year's Eve party you and Nate had planned with those two hot Air France flight attendants."

"I thought about it a time or two," Donovan was surprised to hear himself saying. He was always more circumspect, having learned to carefully weigh his words when he was a Portland patrolman because cops with runaway mouths weren't very likely to rise through the ranks. And they damn well didn't get invited to join the elite FBI. Which had been another of the reasons he'd gone along with Nate and Tess's idea to come to the island. He'd hoped that the bright, tropical sunshine might burn off the fog dulling his brain.

Lani didn't appear to take offense. "What a relief to know that the outspoken Donovan Quinn I remember so well is lurking somewhere inside that funeral suit. I was afraid rubbing elbows with all those politicians and cable news talking heads might have ruined you."

"I haven't changed that much," he insisted, knowing it to be another lie. Sometimes lately, he found himself wondering if the rookie cop who had crawled through those dark and threatening shadows in that warehouse so many years ago even existed any longer. "I'm still just a cop."

"You're a detective who could well end up chief of the department," Lani corrected. "Nate told me all about you tracking down that Cascades Killer. And he also mentioned, when he and Tess were down here for Thanksgiving, that you'd nearly gotten killed while working to keep a Russian mobster in prison."

"I wasn't injured that badly. Some glass in my eye, bumps and bruises. And a sprained ankle." Which was taking its own sweet time getting back to full strength. "And it never would've happened if I'd just moved faster."

She tilted her head. "Gracious, I had no idea being a detective required superpowers capable of outrunning an SUV."

She still had a smart mouth. As he found himself wondering if it would taste as good as it looked, Donovan firmly reminded himself that this was his best friend's sister. Still, one thing Nate hadn't embellished was the beauty of at least one of the island's women.

She picked up her hammer and slid it into a loop on the tool belt she wore low on her hips. "Why don't I come down so we can continue this conversation without you getting a crick in your neck?"

As he steadied the ladder, Donovan decided watching Nate's sister's butt, as she deftly backed down the aluminum steps, was definitely off-limits.

"You're not in the market for a wife, by any chance, are you?" she asked as she reached the ground. She yanked the elastic band from around the knot, allowing a cloud of sunset hair to tumble over her bare shoulders. When she took off the oversized sunglasses, he found himself drowning in her mermaid-green eyes.

"Absolutely not." Realizing how that swift rejection might have sounded, he backtracked. "It's just that my life is complicated, and in flux right now and I don't believe I could give a relationship the time and energy..."

Hell, if he'd stumbled around for words that badly during all those Cascades Killer's press conferences, the FBI never would have come calling. His only excuse, as lame as it admittedly might be, was that it had been a very long time since he'd been with a woman capable of muddling his thoughts and tangling his tongue.

"Don't panic," she said, gilt lights sparkling in those remarkable eyes. "I was merely curious about whether or not you were in on Nate's devious plot."

"Plot?" He rubbed the spot between his brows where a headache had begun to throb.

"My brother has been threatening to marry me off," she said conversationally. As she bent to pick up one of the pieces of luggage, the cutoff jeans rode up enticingly, momentarily capturing his attention with the backs of smooth, tanned thighs. "He obviously sent you down here as bait."

"I seriously doubt he'd do that," Donovan objected. "Here, let me take those."

"I've got them," she said as she headed toward the door. "You bring the large bag and that other case. Which, please tell me isn't a computer."

"It's a new laptop. I figured I'd use the peace and quiet to get some work done."

"You came here to work?" Lani's incredulous expression suggested that he'd confessed to plans to settle beneath the banyan tree in the front yard and spend his holiday vacation watching Internet porn.

"Something wrong with that?"

"Everyone's entitled to his own idiosyncrasies, I suppose." She stopped and glanced back over her shoulder to give him a slow, appraising look. "Nate's told me all about you, Donovan."

"He did?" Donovan racked his brain for something, anything, Nate knew that he might inadvertently let slip during an FBI background investigation.

"Oh, don't worry," she said, apparently picking up on his concern. "According to my brother, you're intelligent, honest, and a terrific judge of literature." She flashed him a quick but still devastating female smile that took him back to high school when just the sight of Madison Mayhue crossing her legs across the aisle during first-period English class could give him a boner that would last until lunch. "That last is because you read all his books, of course."

"He's a great storyteller."

"You don't have to convince me. After he sent me the advance copy of *Nighthawk*, I locked my doors every night for a month."

He frowned. "You don't now?"

"This isn't Portland, Donovan," Lani replied mildly. "We're not accustomed to much crime here on Orchid Island."

"True, but..." His voice trailed off, and he forced an abashed smile. "Sorry. That was the cop talking."

"I suppose, given your line of work, you could develop a jaded view of the world after a while," Lani murmured.

"Or a realistic one," he countered, even as her words hit a bull's-eye, making him aware of the fact that she wasn't the only one who'd changed since that long-ago winter. "So what other deep, dark secret about my personal life has your brother let out of the bag?"

"He said you've become a driven workaholic who needs to relearn how to relax. Tess, by the way, agreed with his assessment."

"Which is a classic case of the pot calling the kettle black," he muttered, a little annoyed that he'd apparently been a topic of conversation during Nate and Tess's visit.

"My soon-to-be sister-in-law was wound a little tightly when she first arrived," Lani allowed. "But it didn't take all that long for her to slip into island time. Watch that third step," she warned as she continued toward the front door. "It's loose. I was going to nail it down after I put in the skylight."

"You're putting in a skylight?"

"Nate suggested one when he asked me to do the remodel." She entered the house, leaving him to follow. Zeroing in on the orchid tattoo rising from the waist of those cutoffs, he wondered how low that ink might go. "He didn't tell me why he needed it done right away, especially since he and Tess are spending Christmas at her family's winery, but as soon as I saw you struggling up the beach, I knew what my sneaky brother had in mind. He's obviously selected you to rescue me from a lonely, celibate spinsterhood."

"Nate only offered this place out of friendship," Donovan assured her even as he wondered how celibate an existence any woman who looked like Lani Breslin could possibly be leading. Nate hadn't mentioned that all the males on the island were blind.

"Not that you haven't grown into a remarkably attractive woman," he said sincerely, as they entered the open-concept home that, to his uneducated design eye, appeared to be a fusion of casual beach living and Asian Zen, punctuated with native carvings and bright art. "But I'm not in the market to get married right now."

"Damn. There goes my big plan to go wedding dress shopping tomorrow. And I guess it also means we won't be picking out a china pattern anytime soon."

She crossed the wood floor scattered with sisal rugs. "Don't worry," she assured him, "we're in full agreement on the topic. Although I think we're in the minority these days. Even my best friend has fallen victim to the matrimonial bug.

"I'm going to be maid of honor at her ceremony at the Fern Grotto next June, and when she throws that orchid bouquet, I'm definitely going to duck. Not that I actually believe in that old wives' tale of the woman who catches the bouquet becoming the next to wed, but there's no point in taking any unnecessary chances, is there?"

She opened a door and waved a graceful hand in a sweeping gesture around the bedroom. "Well, welcome to Shangri-La."

Donovan came to an abrupt halt in the doorway of the bedroom as he took in the tall, four-poster king-size bed. Draped in mosquito netting from the vaulted ceiling to the floor, the bed dominated the room. A broad beam of buttery sunshine from the overhead skylight Lani had mentioned installing cast a soft sheen on a leopard throw tossed across the end of the white sheets. The silvery sound of water tumbling over the lava stones, drew his attention to a waterfall fountain surrounded by lush, tropical green plants in a far corner of the vast room. Moroccan hammered lanterns and large, patterned pillows had been strategically placed on the dark teak floor, inviting occupants of the room to lounge in front of the fountain.

"It's certainly...inviting," he said, taking in the sybaritic scene.

"That's exactly what Nate had in mind," Lani said dryly. "Watch this." She crossed the room and pushed a button, causing bamboo blinds to open and reveal a folding wall of glass that opened to a tropical outdoor rain shower surrounded by yet more plants. Beyond the shower, turquoise water lapping onto coral sand enhanced the unabashed sensuality of the room's decor.

Blaming the erotic atmosphere for his runaway imagination, Donovan found himself wondering if Lani's breasts, barely concealed by the flowered bikini top, were as tanned as the visible parts of her body. Then rigidly tamped down lustful thoughts of moonlight skinny-dipping in the lagoon.

"Would you like to know when he requested this little rush remodeling job?" Before he could venture a guess, she answered her own question. "Ten days ago. I've been working like a demon in order to get everything done on time."

"You did all this?"

"I'm something of a local handyman in my spare time," she said offhandedly. "By the way, the fur is definitely fake. I put my foot down at killing animals just so my brother could create a tropical version of the Playboy Mansion."

She stuck her hands in her back pockets as she looked around the room. "I did all this with my own two hands at Nate's request, never realizing that I was setting the scene for my own seduction."

The sight of her sea-green, thickly lashed eyes and full, lushly inviting lips the hue of a ripe peach, caused an unbidden and inappropriate image of her lying beneath him on the gauze- draped bed to flash on a huge flat-screen in his mind. "You really are mistaken about my reason for being here," he said.

Lani eyed him consideringly. "Oh, I believe you when you say you're here in order to get some work done. But believe *me*, Nate has entirely different plans for us."

He shook his head. "Do all the Breslins have such vivid imaginations?"

She waved away his protest. "I'll explain later. Right now, I need a shower, and you need to get out of those city clothes. I'll run over to my place and meet you back here in an hour."

"Your place?"

"Right around the bend." Lani pointed out the window to the beach. "Handy, isn't it?" she said dryly. "Although I stocked the kitchen for you, it seems only right that I should play a proper hostess by taking you out for dinner. But you don't have to worry." Soothing him with an indulgent smile, she placed a slender hand on his arm. "I have no intention of setting any feminine traps for you, Donovan Quinn. So, you're perfectly safe with me."

With that, she was gone, leaving Donovan to stare out the expanse of glass, admiring the sway of her hips in those faded cutoffs. Glancing down at the spot where her coral polish-tipped fingers had rested briefly on his arm, he imagined he could still feel the heat.

Despite her reassuring words, Donovan had an uneasy feeling that he knew exactly how Adam must have felt when Eve had suddenly shown up in Paradise.

2

L ANI HADN'T ALWAYS lived on Orchid Island. She had, before returning to the island, lived for six years in Los Angeles, where you couldn't throw a stick on a beach without hitting a hot guy. It hadn't taken her that long to become immune to flawlessly straight Hollywood white teeth, sexily shaggy sun-streaked hair, and toned-to-the-nth-degree-of-perfection bodies. So how was it that the too-thin, exhausted-looking Donovan Quinn could, after all these years, still make her go weak at the knees while other, more significant parts had definitely leaped to attention?

The same way they had that first time she'd seen him. It wasn't that she hadn't had crushes before. She'd even taped magazine photos of Joshua Jackson, the poster bad-boy-turned-good from *Dawson's Creek*, onto her bedroom mirror frame and had practiced writing Lani Jackson in her journal. Over and over again.

But a crush on a TV character was a whole lot safer than the way Donovan Quinn had made her feel. Just looking at him in that blue uniform with the big, dangerous gun strapped to his hip had taught her what actual, real life lust felt like. In a desperate attempt to hide her tangled, confused teenage emotions, she'd hidden them behind a mask of petulant hostility.

Proving current appearances deceiving, according to her brother, Donovan was on the fast track. Whether he ended up in the FBI, on some Homeland Security task force, or even, as she could easily see him, Portland Chief of Police, the chances of him staying on the island were about the same as the volcanic Mt. Waipanukai erupting on Christmas Eve.

As were the chances of her ever moving off island again.

So, the question was…now that Nate had thrown them together again, did she follow her heart (which had apparently hung on to that long-ago crush as if it were a virus it hadn't quite shaken off) and those awakened body parts?

Or her head, which was sternly reminding her that any chance of a long-term relationship was slim-to-none?

Fortunately, Lani decided, unless a crime spree needing Detective Donovan Quinn's attention suddenly broke out in Oregon, the man wasn't going anywhere right away. And neither was she.

● ● ●

ALTHOUGH HIS BODY felt as if it had just finished a triathlon, and his ankle was throbbing, Donovan took the time to hang up his clothes before taking a shower and shaving. The shave might have been a mistake, since getting rid of the dark stubble revealed a pallor that reminded him of the faces of lifers he'd sent off to the Oregon State Penitentiary.

The bathroom had come equipped with shampoo, body and face soap, along with toothpaste and extra brushes. Making a mental note to pay Lani back for whatever she'd spent on the bath and well-stocked kitchen, he debated taking a nap and knew from experience the buzzing, like a hive of angry wasps, would start up in his brain again, the same way it did whenever he tried to sleep.

Churned up and edgy, he wandered outdoors. Unable to sit down, he stood on the beach and watched the wavelets rolling in to kiss the sand. As the setting sun turned the sky to apricot and the sea to beaten gold, he tried to remember the last time he'd allowed himself to relax and came up blank.

There'd been a helluva lot to deal with the past few years. A divorce, hunting down the Cascades Killer, investigating Tess's money-laundering case, along with the legal appeal of the Russian mobster she'd been determined to keep in prison, not to mention trying to uncover her stalker. Add in being hit by the driver of that SUV who'd tried to kill him, leaving him with this damn gimpy ankle, and it was no wonder he'd been walking a very thin razor's edge.

Then, just when he could see a light at the end of the criminal tunnel, he'd shown up at his partner's apartment with a six-pack and plans to watch the Seahawks-Forty Niners' game only to find the dull beige wall behind the ratty, thrift store recliner splattered with blood and brains.

Donovan didn't give a flying fuck what his chief, the department shrink, and the chaplain said. Matt Osborne, who, next to Nate, had been the closest thing he'd had to a brother, had been wallowing in a world of pain, and Donovan hadn't recognized how bad the problem had become.

Whenever he and Matt would talk about the Cascades Killer case, their conversations had revolved around the investigation, then working with the district attorney's office to prepare a slam-dunk case for trial. They'd never talked about the victims. The fathers, the mothers, and, God help them, those poor innocent kids who hadn't done anything but gone on a family camping trip. Something his late partner had been deprived of when his ex-wife had returned to her hometown in North Carolina with their children.

Like most police departments, the Portland Police Bureau was populated with men and women who fit into the tough-guy mold that had existed long before Donovan had been born. Cops don't cry. That was the unspoken code. Which ignored the unsavory fact that as many, if not more, cops died by their own gun as they did in the line of duty.

Although many cities, including his own, were getting better about tackling that outwardly strong, silent culture, the truth remained that suicide had long been the black sheep in the blue police family.

Donovan was back to beating himself up over the fact that despite being a hot shot detective, he hadn't caught the clues of his own partner's downward spiral when Lani came around the cove, appearing like something from a fairy tale.

Her hair, gilded by the last rays of the sun and fanned by the soft trade winds, was adorned with a bright yellow blossom. A strapless dress covered with bright tropical flowers bared her sun-kissed shoulders and skimmed her body enticingly, the full skirt billowing around her legs as she walked toward him, a pair of red sandals in her hand.

Revealing he wasn't quite dead yet himself, a spark of heat inside Donovan flickered. When she reached the bottom of the steps, stopped, and smiled, the flicker flamed up. Which was definitely problematic. Because after months of living like a monk, the female who'd started his juices flowing again was the wrong damn woman. Seducing the sister of his best friend was absolutely against the Bro Code.

Lani didn't need to be a detective to catch that spark of interest. One he'd quickly and rigidly banked. Too tense, she thought. And too sad. And once again, dressed as grimly as his expression. Granted, he'd changed out of the charcoal-gray business suit, but the tan slacks and black silk T-shirt were still a far cry from appropriate beach attire. As her eyes moved to his feet, she supposed the supple Italian loafers were his attempt at informality and wondered what had happened to those raggedy old Nikes he'd practically lived in while off duty.

"Don't you own anything casual?"

He lifted a brow. "What's wrong with this?"

"In the first place, those shoes have to go. No one, I repeat, *no one*, wears leather shoes on Orchid Island."

"I'm not accustomed to running with the pack."

His words fit that young cop she'd crushed on. Even as Lani wondered if it were possible to remain independent while rising within such a structured, military-based law-enforcement system, she had to give him credit for the way he avoided sounding unbearably egocentric, the way most men of his accomplishments invariably would.

"That's undoubtedly true. And what you're wearing is a huge improvement over your earlier suit. But you still need work. What time tomorrow do you want to go shopping?"

"Shopping?"

"For clothes. Honestly, Donovan, you can't possibly hope to enjoy yourself dressed like an FBI special agent."

"I'm not a special agent. Yet," he qualified. "I also learned early in my career that the proper clothing encourages respect."

"If you need to dress like a Wall Street trader in order to earn respect, you're probably in trouble."

"Want to guess how far I'd get questioning the business partner of a billionaire commercial real estate developer I know beyond a doubt killed his wife, but can't yet prove it, while wearing a hoodie, torn jeans, and Chucks?" he countered.

"Point taken," she allowed. "But you can't deny that the Italian suit you showed up in looks a lot better on television than the T-shirt and faded jeans I remember you wearing."

His dark blue eyes became as shuttered as windows painted black. Lani supposed he'd developed that distant, detached expression in order to keep suspects from reading his thoughts. In a way, Lani couldn't help but admire that skill. She'd never been all that successful hiding her feelings. Which was partly what had led to her life getting so turned upside down during her time on the mainland.

"I didn't realize you'd been paying so much attention to my attire back then," he said. "In fact, I got the impression that you couldn't stand to be in the same room with me."

Lani shrugged. "I may not have liked you," she admitted. Which wasn't the whole truth and nothing but the truth. What she hadn't liked was the dizzying, unfamiliar way he'd made her feel. "But I never said that you weren't good-looking back then," she said. "You're still a very attractive man, but if clothes really do make the man, as the saying goes, you're not nearly as open or natural as you were back then."

"Are you suggesting I've turned into a phony?"

Lani reminded herself that this man was, after all, her brother's best friend. The least she could do was show a little aloha spirit.

"I'm sorry. I don't know what's gotten into me."

"You've probably had a long day," he suggested. "What with that rush remodeling job Nate dumped on you."

"That's probably it," Lani muttered, not wanting to contradict him, for that would entail admitting that something about Donovan Quinn still put her nerves, and other, more vital parts of her body, uncharacteristically on edge. She fell silent as they both stared out over the turquoise water.

"Nate assured me that this was the ideal place to unwind," Donovan said at length.

"And you need to unwind." It was not a question.

"Is it that obvious?" He held up a hand. "Never mind. You needn't bother answering. I don't know if my ego could take any more battering right now."

"Most people who arrive here from the mainland need a little decompression time," she said mildly. "It's not always easy going from warp speed to island time. I certainly had to go through a major mental adjustment when I returned home from California, which is probably one of the more laid-back states...Meanwhile, I hope you're hungry."

"I think I am."

He sounded surprised. Which, in itself wasn't all that surprising, considering how much weight he'd shed. She wondered why the hell Nate hadn't warned her that not only was Donovan coming to the island, he was arriving both physically and emotionally wounded.

"The last thing I ate was a bag of chips on the plane hours ago. Where are we going?"

"To my parents' house, which is just down the beach. Nate always jokes about this end of the island being the Breslin family compound. Tonight is something of a

command performance for me, and since I didn't think my
brother would want me leaving you alone your first night on
the island, I figured the best thing to do would be to take you
along."

"Are you sure they won't mind?"

She looked at him curiously. "Why would they mind?"

He shrugged. "Well, if it's a special occasion—"

"Don't worry," she told him. "It's only another one of
Daddy's unveiling ceremonies. He assures me that he's created yet another masterpiece."

"Last time I was here, your father was a doctor," he said
as they walked along the hard-packed sand at the edge of the
water. She'd stayed barefoot, while he'd kept his loafers on.
A mistake, he realized as the familiar ache started in again.
He probably should have kept up with those range-of-motion
exercises his doctor had prescribed, but after Matt had eaten
his gun, even getting out of bed had proven an effort.

"He still is. One of those old-fashioned family practitioners. Oh, look!" She pointed up at the top of a jagged cliff
rising inland. Shrouded in silver mist, it was softened by the
touch of a rainbow. "Make a wish."

"Why?"

"Because of the rainbow, of course." She closed her eyes.
"Hurry, before it disappears."

Feeling more than a little foolish, Donovan found himself
doing as she'd instructed. Unfortunately, closing his eyes had
him missing the wave that filled his shoes with wet sand.

"There," she said with satisfaction, opening her eyes
again. "I feel lucky tonight. I hope you wished for something
wonderful, Donovan, because I just know it will come true."

"I thought it was the first star people wished on."

"That only happens once a day," she explained blithely. "If you wish on rainbows, sometimes you get a chance for two or three wishes every day. The odds are much better."

Before he could respond to that idea, a huge beast the size of a small horse came bounding down the hard-packed sand, a long pink tongue lolling from its mouth. A moment later, the beast, which turned out to be a boisterous Harlequin Great Dane, stood on his hind legs, his huge paws braced on Lani's bare shoulders as he joyfully licked her face.

"Meet Horatio," she said, appearing unperturbed as she brushed wet sand off the front of her dress. "Horatio, this is Mr. Quinn. He's a very good friend of Nate's, so I want you to treat him like one of the family."

She bent and picked up a piece of driftwood, throwing it into the water. Horatio took off after it, barking enthusiastically.

"He's spoiled rotten, of course," she said as they watched the dog splashing in the surf as he retrieved the stick. "So you'd best humor him. It's all Daddy's fault."

"He's your father's dog?"

"In a way. You see, Daddy always wanted two sons and two daughters, but mother felt one of each should be enough for any family. Especially when the two children in question were so amazingly exemplary."

"You won't get any argument from me on that point."

"Thank you, Donovan." She flashed him a pleased smile. "That was precisely what you were supposed to say. Anyway," she said, picking up the threads of the story, "a few months ago, Daddy rescued Horatio from the animal shelter.

"He's adopted," she said under her breath as the huge black-and-white animal came bounding back, the stick between his wide jaws. "But no one has had the heart to tell him. He's really very sensitive."

"He's also a dog."

"True, though he doesn't seem to realize that. While I don't entirely agree with Daddy on the subject, I respect his right to keep the facts of Horatio's adoption from him. For the time being." Lani reached down and patted the happily panting dog on the head. "After all, he is only a puppy. When he's older, he'll be able to understand much better."

Donovan searched her face for a hint of humor and found none. He wondered why Nate had never told him that his sister was slightly off-kilter. Then, thinking of Nate Breslin, living in a haunted house with the ghost of a sea captain for a roommate while he wrote lurid tales about things that go bump in the night, Donovan realized Nate might have never noticed. The Breslin family apparently had a looser standard than most when it came to normalcy. Which was why he never would've predicted Lani's older brother and law-and-order, by-the-book Tess Lombardi would be such a perfect fit.

"I won't say a thing," Donovan agreed as they approached a sprawling, three-story white island-style plantation house overlooking the water. It was lit up with so many white Christmas lights, he wouldn't have been surprised if planes mistook the roof for a runway.

"You're still a very nice man, Donovan," she said. "I think I just may forgive my brother for sending you down here to seduce me, after all."

Standing on her toes, which she'd polished the same shiny coral as her fingernails, she brushed her lips against his. Donovan felt a flash of heat and flame before she broke the all-too-brief contact.

"Blue, I think," she mused aloud.

"Blue?"

"The shirt we're going to buy you tomorrow. Blue will do very nicely. A deep sapphire shade to match your eyes. Of course you know that they're quite remarkable."

While he might not be comfortable talking about himself, Lani's candor was refreshing. In his business, most women he met were cops, lawyers, or ones he'd arrested. None of whom were so openly expressive. "Are they?"

"Of course they are," she said, tossing her auburn head as they walked up the steps to the broad, covered front porch. "For heaven's sake, Donovan, an intelligent man, especially one who's received national attention, has certainly taken time to enumerate his strengths and weaknesses. And even when you're carrying all that heavy baggage beneath them, the way you are now, your eyes are one of the most striking things about you."

She paused and leaned forward to study them more closely, her gaze narrowed thoughtfully. "They remind me of the sea at midnight, beneath a full moon."

When she gave him another of those slow smiles, heat collected at the base of his spine.

"I think that this could be a very interesting vacation," he said.

"Or a long one, at any rate," she countered in a dry tone.

3

"WELL, WELL," a feminine voice said. "I see you've brought along another art lover for the unveiling."

Lani tilted her head back, her eyes smiling into Donovan's.

"Mother," she said, not taking her gaze from his, "look who's come to visit us."

Donovan looked past Lani to the woman standing in the open doorway. As tall and lean as her daughter, she had the same sea-green eyes. Unlike Lani's wild reddish mane, however, her jet-black hair flowed down her back like a rippling waterfall, brightened here and there by brilliant streaks of silver.

"What a lovely surprise." The woman's caftan was every bit as colorful as the sundress worn by her daughter, and, like Lani, she smelled like the flowers printed on the flowing material. Donovan felt as if he'd stumbled into a tropical garden.

"It's a pleasure to see you again, Mrs. Breslin," he said.

Kalena Breslin's brightly interested eyes moved from Donovan to her daughter and back again. "The pleasure is ours, Donovan. But please, although it's been too long since you visited, we're friends, so I insist you call me Kalena. Nate was telling us all about your success when he was here with Tess for Thanksgiving."

"Nate sent Donovan down here to seduce me," Lani offered.

"Your brother has always been an enterprising man," Kalena agreed easily. "In that respect he takes after your father."

Donovan felt obliged to set the record straight. "Lani's mistaken."

Kalena smiled, the same slow, devastating smile that made her daughter so dangerous. "I'm not so sure," she said smoothly. "My daughter has always been quite perceptive." She glanced at Lani. "By the way, Taylor called here looking for you, sounding upset. I told her you'd call her back as soon as you arrived."

"Taylor Young is my friend who's getting married at the grotto," Lani explained to Donovan. "She's been floating on clouds ever since they got engaged. I wonder what could be wrong," she murmured, more to herself than to her mother or Donovan. "I let my cell die again. I'll have to call her on your landline before dinner."

"From the way she sounded, I believe you should," Kalena agreed. "You don't think she and Ford might be having problems regarding the wedding?"

Lani shook her head decisively. "Not a chance. I've never seen a couple as wild about each other as Taylor and Ford." She smiled up at her mother. "Except you and Daddy, of course."

Kalena grinned at that. "What a nice thing to say," she enthused. "And so very true."

She moved aside, gesturing them into the house. The wood entry floor was covered in hemp-textured rugs, and track lighting along the ceiling illuminated the vivid paintings crowding high white walls. All were island scenes, the subjects varying from sun-dappled landscapes to formal portraits to colorful abstracts. The only thing the works of art had in common was that they were undeniably terrible. It was all Donovan could do not to stop and stare.

"Did you warn Donovan about the showing?" Kalena asked Lani as they wound their way down a long hallway lined with more canvases.

"I started to, but I got distracted by a rainbow."

"Oh, dear," Kalena murmured regretfully. "I missed that one."

She glanced up at Donovan, whose attention had been momentarily captured by a portrait of a young native girl seated in the surf beside a wind-tossed palm. Had she stood up, Donovan would have bet she'd have topped the tree by at least ten feet. He vaguely remembered seeing the portrait's twin in the airport terminal.

"I do hope you made a good wish, Donovan," Kalena said. "Evening rainbows are especially lucky."

His eyes moved to Lani's. And held for a long, humming moment. "I certainly hope so."

Kalena nodded, seemingly satisfied. "Good. Now about Thomas's painting," she said briskly. "It undoubtedly has not escaped your notice that my husband, while being a delightful and intelligent man, as well as a wonderful physician, possesses absolutely no talent whatsoever."

"His style is definitely unusual," Donovan offered, trying not to offend.

"You don't have to mince words," Lani said. "My father and I just happen to be the only two individuals in this family who managed to be out to lunch when talent was being passed out. Unfortunately, while I accepted that fact long ago, Daddy continues to delude himself with the idea that he's another Gauguin."

"You're quite talented, darling," Kalena argued. "None of my friends' children have nearly as many college degrees as you do. And everyone loves what you've done to the house."

"Poor Mother." Lani shook her head in mock despair. "She just can't accept the fact that she gave birth to a child with absolutely no marketable artistic abilities."

Kalena Breslin's words reminded Donovan of Nate's saying that Lani had stayed in school much longer than the average student, gathering a bouquet of degrees in history, comparative literature, philosophy, and library science.

"Design is definitely a talent," Kalena countered. "One I've no doubt you could be very successful at if you ever decided to do it professionally."

"Then it would become a job. Not fun," Lani argued.

Her mother's slight sigh suggested they'd had this conversation before. "At any rate, Donovan, my husband enjoys his little fantasy." Her shoulders lifted in a graceful shrug. "So we all indulge him."

"*All* meaning the entire island," he guessed, thinking back on the painting in the airport. Surely hanging it in a public place had to have required official approval.

"Of course," Lani broke in. "Daddy's treated everyone on Orchid Island at one time or another. Everybody adores him, so whenever he has a showing, people show up and buy out the gallery."

Donovan tried to imagine such a communal act of subterfuge taking place in Portland, or even Honolulu, and found it highly unlikely. He felt as if his plane had somehow gone off course on the way from Oʻahu and landed in Oz.

"Don't worry, Donovan." Kalena's laugh was deep and throaty as she patted his cheek. "No one expects you to buy anything."

"Unless you want to," Lani hinted broadly. "Who knows, Donovan, you might actually fall in love with Daddy's latest artistic effort and simply have to have it."

"It's Lani's turn to take a painting home," Kalena explained.

"Well, I don't think it's fair," Lani muttered, hands on her hips. "Just because I live on the island, I have to hang the stuff on my walls. Nate stores his in the back of his closets."

"You don't know that for a fact, darling."

Lani shot a spear-like look straight at Donovan, who'd been trying to stay out of the dispute. "You've visited Nate at Sunset Point, haven't you?"

"Several times."

"So have you seen any Thomas Breslin paintings hanging around my brother's haunted house?"

"No," he admitted. "But I'm sure there's a good reason."

She folded her arms. "Name one."

"Perhaps the captain took them."

Lani snorted at that idea, while her mother appeared genuinely interested. "Oh, have you met Nate's ghost friend, Donovan?"

Donovan was not nearly as surprised by the question as he might have been a few hours earlier. After hearing the story of Horatio, he had made the decision to simply go with the flow and not attempt to analyze anything having to do with this family whom he was beginning to remember being the most colorful he'd ever met. Which, having grown up with two workaholic, serious-minded parents, had left him envious of his best friend.

"No. He turned out to be pretty reclusive. At least during the times I was there."

"I suppose I can understand that," Kalena mused. "However, it's not exactly the behavior you'd expect from a sea captain, now, is it? One would expect such a man to be far bolder and expansive."

They had reached a set of sliding doors that led to a flower-filled, glass-walled sunroom dominated by a towering Christmas tree covered with poinsettias and yet more white lights. At their arrival, an enormous orange cat sleeping on a bamboo chair lifted her head. Obviously deciding they weren't worth the effort it would take to wake up, she closed her amber eyes and dismissed them by flicking her striped tail over her nose.

"Lani!" A tall, silver-haired man—who gave Donovan the idea of what Nate would look like when he was older—rose from a wicker throne chair and came toward them, his tanned face wreathed in a welcoming smile. Backing up his daughter's claim about casual dress being appropriate dinner attire, he was wearing a pair of drawstring white cotton pants, flip-flops, and a purple shirt printed with palm trees and coconuts.

"You're a vision of loveliness tonight," Thomas Breslin said as he wrapped his arms around Lani in a bear hug, as if it had been months since he'd seen her. Lani had often thought that while she'd inherited her looks from her mother, her natural exuberance—which her last year in L.A. had nearly knocked out of her—had come from this man's DNA.

After he'd released her, his eyes narrowed thought-fully. "I do believe I'll paint you, my dear, wearing that very dress." He rubbed his chin. "We'll want the correct light, of course. Sunrise, I should think." He nodded with satisfaction. "Definitely sunrise. It'll bring out the fire in your hair."

"You know how much I adore you, Daddy," Lani said, "but if you expect me to pose for you before noon, you're crazy."

"Humph." He turned his attention to Donovan. "What do you think?" he demanded. "Aren't I right? She should be painted with the first fingers of dawn rising over her shoulder."

"And her titian hair blowing free in the wind, like a way-ward sea sprite," Donovan agreed.

"Exactly." Lani's father leaned forward, lifting her hair in soft clouds that drifted over her bare shoulders.

"Father," she said sternly as she backed away, "that's enough for now." Lani was uncomfortable having the two men discuss her as if she were nothing more than some inani-mate object he intended to paint. She'd seen her father look that same way at a pear. Or a tree. Or a fish, during his island marine life stage.

"It's good to see you again, Dr. Breslin," Donovan said.

"And you, my boy." Having always been a toucher, Thomas ignored the outstretched hand, giving Donovan an effusive, one-arm guy lean-in hug that ended with three manly pats on the back. "You've stayed away too long."

"It's been awhile," Donovan agreed. "I'm afraid time got away from me while I found myself caught up in life."

"He's become a workaholic," Lani divulged.

"Nate suggested that was the case when he and the lovely Tess were here for Thanksgiving," Thomas said. "Well, we'll just have to break you of unfortunate habits." Lani watched a line etch its way across Donovan's forehead and suspected he was getting tired of people criticizing his work.

"Did you paint the woman in the airport?" he asked in a less-than-subtle attempt to shift the topic away from himself.

"Saw the painting, did you?" Thomas said with obvious pride. "What did you think?"

"I can honestly say I've never seen anything like it."

Lani hadn't realized that she'd been holding her breath until she exhaled a sigh of relief and gave Donovan an appreciative smile.

"I like this one," Thomas announced. "Where have you been hiding him, Lani?"

"Portland," she answered absently, her eyes moving toward the draped easel in the corner. It was so big. Why couldn't her father take up painting miniatures? "Nate sent him to me for Christmas."

Thomas nodded in much the same manner his wife had, on hearing the news. "Your brother always did have good taste in gifts...No peeking!"

Thomas's deep voice boomed suddenly, causing Lani to jerk her fingers away from the edge of the white sheet. "We'll have the unveiling in due course. After dinner. A little suspense will heighten the appreciation. In the meantime, after you call your friend, why don't you help your mother in the kitchen, my dear, while your young man and I discuss the merits of early morning light."

He put his arm around Donovan's shoulder, leading him over to the pair of chairs. "Tallulah, it's time for you to join the ladies in the kitchen," he instructed firmly.

The orange tabby opened one yellow eye and looked up at him, apparently unmoved by his request.

"Come along, dear," Kalena coaxed, "we're having opakapaka baked in banana leaves tonight, and I saved back a bit of the fish fillet just for you."

She'd apparently said the magic word. The cat stretched in a slow, fluid movement, then jumped lightly onto the floor and followed the two women out of the room.

"Tallulah's a good girl," Thomas said, watching the cat leave. "But stubborn. When she digs her claws in, she can give Lani a run for her money, and Lord knows, that one has been known to try a man's patience from time to time."

Of that, Donovan had not a single doubt. "So you think of her as another daughter?" After what Lani had told him about Thomas Breslin's desire for two sons and two daughters, if the man was off-center enough to consider Horatio the second son he'd never had, he assumed Lani's father would think of the huge orange cat as an equal member of the family.

"How crazy do you think we Breslin's are?" Thomas's face registered surprise. "While she may steadfastly refuse to admit it, Tallulah's a cat."

4

THE ART-UNVEILING DINNER turned out to be what Lani told him was Hawai'ian pink snapper, thin slices of gold potatoes, tomato, cabbage, pepper, carrots, herbs, and butter wrapped in banana leaves, then baked in a salted crust.

Using a silver hammer, Thomas cracked the crust open with a decidedly theatrical flair. As he unwrapped the banana leaves, the rich, herb-fragrant steam that escaped caused Donovan's appetite, which had been missing in action for weeks, to spike.

"This is delicious," he said after taking a bite from the plate put in front of him. His taste buds, which had also been on hiatus, were practically doing the tango on his tongue.

"I'm glad you're enjoying it," Kalena said with a warm smile.

"I definitely am." And wasn't that an understatement? It was all Donovan could do not to lick his plate.

"Mother's a fabulous cook," Lani said. "Just wait until you taste her kalua pulled pork at the Christmas luau."

"Luau?"

"After the parade," Thomas told him. "We roast the pig underground, with stones, right here on the beach. It's an Orchid Island tradition you won't want to miss."

"I don't want to intrude."

"That would be difficult," Lani said. "Since practically the entire island shows up for the dinner show."

"Lani's one of the dancers," Kalena said.

That got Donovan's attention. "Are you talking hula?"

"Not the tourism kind with the grass skirt and bikini top you're thinking," Lani said.

"I wasn't thinking anything." Like hell he wasn't.

"It's a *kahiko* hula," Lani told him, with just enough of a smirk to let him know he'd been busted. "The old style with chants and drums, before it became westernized with ukes, steel guitars, and cheesy lyrics."

"Some of the newer songs are quite nice," Kalena said.

"True. But the *kahiko* is not only more authentic, it's also, in my humble opinion, much more entertaining," Thomas said. "They all tell a story. Mostly of local legends. You'll enjoy it."

"You also have to come to the parade," Lani insisted. "Daddy, of course, is always grand marshal, given that he's technically royalty."

"Only because my great-grandmother married into a branch of the old Hawai'ian royal family," Thomas said with what Donovan took to be the same genuine humility that he'd recognized in Nate, even as his friend's publishing career had taken off like a comet. "I only accepted the position because islanders keep voting to maintain tradition, but it's not like I ever declare edicts or make laws."

"Although I've never seen you turn down the opportunity to ride on that head float. And throw the year's biggest luau," Lani said with an indulgent smile. That she loved her family was more than apparent. That they loved her back equally so. Which had Donovan thinking of the strained call he'd be having on December twenty-fifth with his own parents.

As appealing as watching Lani doing any kind of hula would be, Donovan would prefer going skinny-dipping with sharks to attending what he suspected was going to be a noisy, crowded beach bash. But hot shot detective that he was, he'd already determined that Lani wouldn't let him spend the day alone in Nate's beach cottage, eating a frozen turkey dinner and watching some TV bowl game. Also, he didn't want to risk offending Kalena and Thomas Breslin by not taking them up on their invitation.

"Sounds like fun," he said. Right behind having a root canal.

• • •

THE NIGHT GLEAMED silver and black velvet, as stars glistened in an ebony sky and a gentle rain drifted down from indigo clouds scudding across the moon. The intoxicating scent of plumeria, frangipani, and night-blooming jasmine floated on the warm Pacific breeze as sand sparkled like diamonds underfoot.

"I really like your family," Donovan said as he and Lani returned down the beach after dinner.

"They like you, too."

"Even Horatio?" The dog hadn't left Donovan's side the entire time he was at the house.

"Especially Horatio."

"You were pulling my leg with that bit about him being the other son your father never had, weren't you?"

Her eyes sparkled as brightly as the stars overhead as she looked up at him. "Guilty," she admitted, a runaway smile quirking the corners of her lips. "But I had you going for a moment, didn't I?"

"More than a moment. You should have seen your father's face when I asked him if he thought of Tallulah as his daughter."

"You did not!"

"I did," Donovan said. "Causing your father to look at me as if I'd lost my mind."

"I told you not to mention it to him," Lani reminded him. "But you needn't worry. My father's a very tolerant man."

The warm water lapped against their legs as they waded in the foaming surf. She'd been secretly pleased when Donovan had taken off his loafers to join her. Sometime during the day Lani had decided to make Donovan Quinn her new project. She would, she vowed, teach him to relax and learn to enjoy the simpler things in life. And if that included some bumping of happy parts, so much the better.

"And of course my brother thinks you walk on water."

"The feeling's mutual. I've been a fan of his ever since he rode with me researching *The Haunting of Hannah Grimm*."

"My brother has a great many fans. He's choosier about his friends. He has to be."

During those times she'd visited Nate in California, Lani had watched so many insincere industry people fawning over him. Movie studio executives, who saw a gold mine in his vastly popular occult novels, along with starlets, would-be starlets, and established stars, all wanting to be seen out and about with the country's hottest novelist.

Then there were all those entrepreneurs wanting licensing rights for everything from the she-wolf vampire dolls to a Day-glo poster series depicting the savagely avenging spirits of a fictional California serial killer's victims.

Eventually, Nate had left California for Oregon. Which, in turn, had led him to Tess Lombardi.

The ironic thing was that before things had come tumbling down around her, Lani had gradually slid into that Tinseltown mentality. The entire life-changing event had begun during one of those visits to her brother during the filming of one of his novels for which he'd also written the screenplay.

It was at the Sony studio in Culver City, that she'd met a producer of *Jeopardy!*, which just happened to be not only America's favorite game of answers and questions, but hers, as well. After attending a taping, when asked how she had enjoyed the show, Lani had offered a hesitant opinion that the audience, as well as the contestants, was capable of enjoying a wider range of questions. Questions that required additional thought, more depth.

To Lani's astonishment, the producer had invited her to apply as a researcher, which included taking the same test as potential contestants. Passing with flying colors, she'd been hired. Then promoted to a writer less than a year later. Three years after that, she'd been plucked from TV obscurity by a top producer known for over-the-top reality shows.

The concept of *Beauty Tames the Beast* was for a cast of beautiful women to instruct hottie blue-collar guys (who, each week would find various contrived reasons to appear without shirts) on various social graces, such as wardrobe, grooming, and planning romantic dates for the beauties.

Each week there would be two tests, and at the end of the episode, the home audience would vote for which hunks had shown enough potential to continue on for another week.

It had, admittedly, been a long way from *Masterpiece Theater*, but as a rule, in real life, the participants were actually nicer and more intelligent than some of the editing showed. The best part had been creating challenges that would not only entertain but give the men skills they could take back home to the real world. What woman wouldn't love a man to surprise her with a romantic breakfast in bed? One he'd actually made with his two manly hands. Or who could actually discuss, with some authority, the topics of love, class, family, and self-deception in *Pride and Prejudice?*

With the exception of a few male reviewers—whom she'd always suspected were secretly jealous of the hottie cast of firemen, cops, cowboys, fishermen, construction workers, mechanics, and even a movie stuntman—most of the entertainment press recognized *Beauty* as bringing a level of intelligence and behavior not often found in the typical, overly voyeuristic reality-programming genre.

The show also earned an Emmy nomination, and although it ended up losing to *The Amazing Race*, wearing a designer gown and borrowed jewels for the awards show red carpet had made Lani feel like Cinderella. Sans the Prince Charming, since her brother had been her date.

Hired as a junior producer, her actual duties had been that of a contestant wrangler, which she'd enjoyed and had made her feel like a mother hen to a clutch of chicks. Although she'd been too busy working to have time for any serious romantic relationships, if she spent an evening sitting home with a good book, as she usually did, it was by choice, not because of a lack of opportunity.

Eventually, she'd come to realize that her friendships would wax and wane according to her success. In the beginning, those on the rungs above her hadn't noticed her existence, while others who'd been struggling along with her during those early days had drifted away as her star had begun to rise.

After one particularly unsavory public incident, which had been edited out of *Beauty*, Lani had realized how badly her life had slipped out of control. Which was when she'd jumped off that glittery hamster wheel and returned to Orchid Island, reuniting with her old friends, and picking up relationships as if she'd never been away.

"I'm choosy about my friends, as well," he said mildly, breaking into her thoughts about how the smartest thing she'd ever done was to return home. "In my business, I have to be."

With that point silently acknowledged, Lani decided to change the subject. "You don't have to keep the painting," she said. "That was a dirty trick."

"Giving it to me as a welcome-to-Orchid-Island gift?" He surprised her with a boyish grin that showed off amazing dimples and had her wanting to jump him on the spot. An impulse she resisted. "I thought it was inspired."

She laughed, enjoying the moment. Enjoying him. "It was the only thing I could think of. The minute I saw it, I knew I'd simply die if I had to hang it on my wall." She shook her head. "I do wish my father would get over his Picasso period. At least in the old days, his subjects bore some slight resemblance to reality."

"I've also no idea what it's supposed to be," Donovan admitted. Since it was too large to carry, they'd left the brilliant orange-and-red abstract oil painting at the Breslin house. Thomas had promised to have it delivered to the cottage the following day.

"It's supposed to depict the legend of Kealehai."

"I'm still lost."

"It's one of our island's most popular stories," she said. "One day, Kealehai, an ancient goddess of fire who lives in Mt. Waipanukai's volcano, decided to take on a human form and walk among the people. When she reached a beach on the far side of the island, a great ceremony was taking place to honor the eighteenth birthday of Taranga, who was not only a prince of the royal family but had been given the gifts of male beauty and charm by the goddesses who'd attended his birth. As Kealehai watched the festivities, she became captivated by him. Not only was he a stunningly beautiful young man, Taranga was the best dancer she'd ever seen."

"Love at first sight."

"Or at least lust at first sight," Lani agreed dryly. "Especially since, according to legend, she'd gone a century without a human mate."

"Talk about your dry spells."

"I suppose time's not the same when you're in spirit form," Lani suggested. "At any rate, being a very passionate spirit—"

"Which would be expected for a goddess of fire."

"Exactly. Kealehai decided that she had to have him, but there was a slight glitch."

The lazy breeze coming off the water fanned her hair, allowing him to breathe in the fragrant gardenia scent of her shampoo. Hit with a sudden jolt of desire, Donovan slipped his hand into his front pocket to keep from touching her. "A glitch?"

When she stopped to look up at him, moonlight gleaming in her eyes, he wondered if she'd heard the raw need in his voice. "Donovan?"

He knew that if he responded to the soft invitation in her voice, he'd be toast. He'd built his life on a solid foundation of self-control and wasn't about to allow this woman, as enticing as she was, to undermine it in a single day.

"You were telling me about Kealehai," he reminded her, rigidly reining in the impulse to drag her down onto the warm sand and reenact *From Here to Eternity*'s iconic beach lovemaking scene.

"Right." Lani blew out a deep breath, suggesting he wasn't alone in his feelings. "Since she derived her spirit power from the volcano, if they made love on his village's beach, so far away from her own fire pit, her youthful human facade could crumble away and the handsome young man would realize how old she actually was."

"Mature women have their appeal, but it sounds as if she might have been pushing that envelope."

"She was several centuries older than your average cougar," Lani agreed. "So, she put a trance on him long enough to get away. Then, once she got back to the volcano, she sent her younger sister, Marua, to bring him back."

"Did Marua share her sister's heated charms?"

"Actually, she was like the soft moon to Kealehai's blazing sun. Having always lived in her older sister's much brighter shadow, she'd never had an opportunity to know love. Until they were returning from Taranga's village, when suddenly, on impulse, the young prince grabbed her and planted a deep, hot kiss on her. From the way it's described in the various versions of the legend, he would have kissed the socks right off her. If she'd been wearing any at the time."

Donovan so didn't need to be talking about impulsive kissing right now. Especially since Lani was also barefoot. Although he was totally a leg guy, he'd never been into women's feet. Until this moment. "And thus the eternal love triangle," he said.

"It didn't happen right away," Lani said. "And it wasn't as if she invited the kiss. Marua was not only sweet, and a virgin, she was truly loyal to her sister."

"And undoubtedly afraid of her sister's temper," Donovan suggested, having seen more than a few romantic triangles turn deadly.

"Probably so," Lani conceded. "At any rate, Marua insisted that they both remember that he'd already pledged himself to Kealehai. And that should have been that."

"Yet there wouldn't be a legend if the plot hadn't thickened." Donovan didn't need his detective skills to tell that this story was going to end badly.

"You're getting ahead of me," Lani complained. "Having been tempted by her first kiss, Marua hesitantly allowed another. And, as the story goes, being cast under the spell of the prince's magical charm, she even initiated a few kisses herself as they traveled from the beach through the valley.

"Unfortunately, Kealehai had been watching out for the couple from her peak on Mt. Waipanukai high over the island. She became more and more enraged with each kiss she witnessed and literally blew her top just as poor, bewitched Marua arrived back with Taranga.

"When he saw the fiery display of passion, the man-whore of a prince forgot all about poor sweet Marua, swept Kealehai into his arms, and made mad, passionate love to her on the edge of the erupting volcano. Unfortunately, instead of enjoying a lovely afterglow of postcoital bliss, Taranga was incinerated by the flames...And that's the painting you're going to have gracing your wall."

"That's fine with me."

Lani stopped again to stare up at him. "You've got to be kidding. It's one of the ugliest things Daddy's ever done."

Unable to resist touching, he ran his knuckles down her cheek. "Ah, but whenever I look at it, I'll think of you."

In turn, Lani dropped her sandals on the beach and placed her hands on his shoulders. "Are you accusing me of having a temper?"

"No," he murmured, tracing the exquisite planes and hollows of her face with his fingertips, "I'm accusing you of making things very, very warm around here."

"Is that a complaint?" she asked in a soft, breathless voice.

"I don't know."

They stared at each other, both searching for answers as the soft rain continued to fall. Finally, Donovan lifted a few heavy strands of wet hair off her face, bent his head, and brushed her cheek with his lips.

"You taste like rain."

"Liquid sunshine," she said, closing her eyes as his mouth skimmed over her face. "It never rains in paradise, Donovan. Didn't Nate tell you that when he was sending you down here to seduce me?"

"I didn't come here to seduce you."

"Newsflash, Detective." Eyes wide open now, she trailed a fingernail down the front of his T-shirt. "You really wouldn't have to."

"Now who's seducing whom?"

"Does it matter?"

"I think it does." He was drowning here. Drowning in her huge mermaid eyes and warm silky lips he knew he'd be tasting in his sleep. The breeze from the sea was pressing the flowered silk against her body in a way that left very little to his imagination. An imagination that kicked into overdrive as he fantasized about those mile-long legs wrapped around his hips.

"Anyone ever tell you that perhaps, just maybe, you think too much?" she asked. "Not everything has to be so complicated."

She wasn't the first person to tell him that. Most recently her brother and Tess. "It's late," he said quietly as he dropped his hand and took a step back. Literally and figuratively. "And you're getting wet."

"So are you."

He glanced down, surprised to find his own clothing soaked. "It looks better on you."

Her laugh was as silvery as the moonlight streaming over them. Then she flashed him an unaffected smile that jolted him to the core. "We have a saying around here, Donovan: The faster you go, the more you miss along the way."

Rising up on her bare toes, she brushed her lips lightly, tantalizingly against his. "You wouldn't want to miss anything, would you?"

Bending down, she scooped up the sandals she'd dropped and went running up the beach toward her cottage. As the

Pacific trade winds carried her laughter to his ears, Donovan picked up his wet shoes and resumed walking toward Nate's beach house, fighting the urge to follow Lani and continue where they'd left off.

But that would be giving in to impulse, and it had been a very long time since anyone had accused Donovan Quinn of being an impulsive man.

5

THE PHONE, WHICH he'd left on the bedside table, jolted
Donovan from a blazing-hot dream of making love to
Lani on the edge of a volcano. He fumbled for the receiver
without opening his eyes.

"What?"

"So much for Orchid Island filling you with the old aloha
spirit," the deep male voice said with a laugh.

"Aloha spirit be damned," Donovan muttered as he sat
up in bed. "What the hell did you have in mind, anyway?"

"Concerning what?"

Donovan's scowling gaze circled the room. "Your redeco-
rating, for one thing."

"How did it turn out?" Nate inquired interestedly.

"Like something out of an old movie: me Tarzan, you Jane.
For God's sake, Nate, haven't you ever heard of overkill?"

"Sounds like Lani followed my instructions to a T."

Donovan could hear the smile in his best friend's voice.
"Speaking of your sister," he began, not bothering to hide his
belief that Lani had been right about one thing: Nate had
definitely set them up.

Nate's next words confirmed his suspicions. "Isn't she something? Face like a Botticelli angel, figure as sleek as a Thoroughbred, and a spirit to match."

"She told your parents that you sent me down here to seduce her."

"Actually, I sent you down to the island to reboot your personal life, which has pretty much been in the toilet lately. And okay, maybe I hoped Lani might be able to help you lighten up and relax, because that's pretty much what she's always done. Even when she was working on that reality show, she was more about taking emotional care of the contestants than creating on-screen drama.

"As for throwing you guys together, I did have the good sense to run the idea by Tess first, and she agreed it couldn't hurt. So, what are you going to do? Arrest me for wanting to help out a pal?"

"And if I seduce your sister?"

"Believe me, I've seen many guys try and fail. If she does decide to give you a shot, it'll be because she wants to. Not because of any rain shower I had her install...Hold on a second."

Although he partly covered the phone, Donovan could hear Tess's voice in the background.

"Tess says that if you two decide on vacation fling sex, that wouldn't be such a bad thing. But she'd rather go shopping for a wedding gift. Which also works for me and would probably make Mom and Dad really happy. Dad especially because it'd give him a chance to throw a big bash. He loves getting everyone together. When Lani and I were kids, he held a blue moon theme party. He even got Sha Na Na to come to the island and perform the song."

"You're making that up."

"I kid you not. The backup guys showed up in gold lamé, which wasn't exactly beach attire, and Bowzer had even shaved his armpits, which was kind of weird. But the show was retro-cool and everyone loved it."

"I've already gotten invited to the Christmas luau."

"Best party of the year," Nate said. "It even tops Dad's New Year's fireworks extravaganza. Once you see Lani dance, you'll probably propose on the spot."

"I'm not in the market for a wife," Donovan reminded him. "I'm down here recharging for the Academy."

"So you've actually decided to become a Feeb?"

Donovan thought he detected a hint of disapproval in Nate's voice. "Probably. Either that or making chief has been my goal from the beginning."

"Not exactly the beginning," Nate was quick to point out. "I seem to remember spending hours in a patrol car with an idealistic, wet-behind-the-ears rookie who kept spouting off about helping the people, making the world a better place to live in, yada, yada, yada. I often wondered if you didn't get all caught up in climbing that ladder of success to show Kendall she'd made a mistake when she walked out on your marriage."

"Kendall had nothing to do with it," Donovan countered irritably. One thing he didn't need was a lecture about his former wife.

"Didn't she?"

"Not at all," Donovan said. He'd become concerned they'd be a bad fit before the wedding, but both Kendall—whose family had known his forever—and his parents had assured him that pre-wedding doubts were normal. "Besides, what makes you think I won't be in a better position to help people as a special agent?"

"In the first place, those guys seem to live in their own worlds and don't spend all that much personal time mixing with ordinary citizens. You'd be even more socially isolated than you are now."

"I'm not socially isolated." Hadn't he gone out to dinner tonight?

"So you say. There's also the point that Lani would hate the gypsy lifestyle of following you around from field office to field office as you climbed that federal bureaucratic ladder."

"Which is a moot point since she assured me that she's no more interested in getting married than I am."

"Then she's lying either to herself or you...And you must really be getting along like gangbusters to have discussed marriage your first day on the island."

"Only in regards to your passion pit."

"Now see, you've got to be exaggerating, because my sister has excellent taste. She flew up and helped me decorate this house when I moved in. She definitely doesn't do tacky."

"Okay. So, maybe the bedroom is sensual, not tacky. But the fact remains that Lani and I are both single adults, capable of making our own decisions. So, why don't you do us both a big favor and butt out?"

The silence extended so long, Donovan thought his phone had dropped the call. Finally, Nate responded. "From where I'm at, marriage seems like a pretty good institution."

"Says the guy who's never been there," Donovan said. "Look, I'm sincerely happy for you and Tess. You're both great people who deserve each other. But—"

"Did you ever wonder why you've never remarried?" Nate cut in abruptly.

"Maybe because I've been there, done that, and ended up giving away the T-shirt when I got hammered in the property settlement?"

"Well, there is that. But my job is to delve beneath the surface of things."

"You write horror novels."

"I write stories about horrifying things happening to ordinary people," he corrected. "Which means I spend a lot of my life walking in my characters' shoes. And while I hate to dis a pal, you're pretty stereotypical."

"Thanks for the ego boost."

"Just telling it like I see it. Also, having watched you all these years, I've come to the conclusion that the reason you've never really fallen in love is because with the exception of Tess, whom you thankfully let get away before things turned romantic, which gave me the golden chance to snatch her up, you've dated a series of identical, proper, predictable women. Admittedly, they're beautiful and intelligent, but they're all cut from the same boring cookie cutter."

"Thanks for the lecture on my love life," Donovan responded, annoyed when the accusation hit too close to home for comfort. "Now, if you don't mind, I think I'll go back to sleep, and for the sake of our friendship, I'll forget this conversation ever occurred."

"You do that," Nate agreed in an obliging manner. "But, Donovan—"

"What now?"

"You don't have to marry Lani. But don't hurt her." The edge to Nate's voice reminded Donovan that the writer wasn't as easy going as he usually appeared.

"I've no intention of hurting anyone. Least of all your sister."

"Just make damn sure you don't," Nate said seriously. Then he cut off the call before Donovan could respond.

Frustrated, Donovan turned his phone off just as he heard a light tapping at his door. "Now what?"

Tugging on a pair of jeans, he marched into the front room and threw open the screen door.

Damn. His annoyance dissolved like a sandcastle under high tide as he viewed Lani, scantily clad in a bright pink bikini, looking as if she should be served up in a sugar cone. She was wearing a flowered shirt over the bikini but hadn't bothered to button it. At the enticing sight of all that golden flesh, the erotic dream Nate's phone call had interrupted came crashing back.

Lani didn't falter under Donovan's glare. After lying awake all night considering the matter, she'd decided that he was in dire need of a strong dose of fun. And she was going to see that he learned to enjoy himself, whether he wanted to or not.

"Good morning," she said, brushing past him into the beach house. "You seem to have woken up on the wrong side of the bed." The familiar tropical floral scent tantalized as she breezed by him.

"Sorry. Your brother just woke me up."

"I hope you told him that we didn't appreciate his devious plan for you to seduce me. As if we were merely two of his characters he was moving around on that Technicolor screen in his warped writer's mind."

"Not in so many words, but I did tell him that we're capable of handling our own affairs."

"Interesting choice of words," she murmured as she opened a cupboard. "Is that what we're going to have? An affair?"

As she reached up for the mugs on the second shelf, her shirt rose, displaying a weakening amount of tanned hip, causing Donovan's mouth to go dry. "At this point, I'd say that's up to you."

"It's an intriguing idea," she mused aloud as she put the mugs on the counter and took a bag of coffee beans from the freezer. "The only hitch is that I gave up sex for Lent."

"It's been a while since I've been inside a church. But I do remember that Lent ends at Easter."

"Got me there," she admitted cheerfully. "But, as I said last night, time moves at a different pace here on the island. We have another saying that the smiles you collect along the way are more important than the miles covered...

"Meanwhile, I'm going to make you a cup of the best coffee you've ever had. Then after breakfast, I have plans for you."

"Now I'm intrigued."

"Don't get ahead of yourself. At the moment, my plans don't involve tangling any sheets. But we *are* going to get wet."

After the erotic dream Nate had interrupted, the thought of the two of them breaking her sexual fast together was almost more than he could take before coffee.

"You don't have to make me breakfast," he said over the sound of dark beans being ground.

"It's obvious you haven't been eating properly," she said as she put a large glass measuring cup of water in the microwave. "Last night was a start—"

"Your mother's a fantastic cook."

"Isn't she? I can't possibly live up to her kitchen skills, but I make a hell of an omelet." She reached into another cupboard and retrieved a French press.

"Fancy," Donovan said.

"These are peaberry beans," she said. "They deserve royal treatment."

"I thought Kona was the big coffee deal around these islands."

"It is. And it's fine enough. And these are actually Kona, but they're extra special because unlike most beans, which grow together like connected twins, these make up the five-percent that are only children."

She held out the small, round dark bean on the palm of her hand. "Since they get all Mother Nature's attention while growing, they're denser and sweeter. And also more expensive, because there's no way to tell whether you're dealing with doubles or singles inside the coffee cherry. So, each peaberry has to be plucked out by hand. But you'll see that they're worth the price.

"Which, by the way, you don't have to worry about," she said, as she measured the ground beans into the press, "because I charged them to Nate's account. And before you argue about that, may I point out that you are, after all, not only his best friend but his guest, so I know he'd want you to have the very best."

She added boiling water in stages, pressed the plunger to filter the grounds, poured the coffee into a white mug, put it in front of him, and stood there, arms crossed. "So tell me what you think."

As the fragrance rose almost visibly upward, like in those Saturday morning cartoons Donovan had watched when his parents were out of town, he took a taste of the rich, dark brew. "I'm pretty certain I hear angels singing."

"I told you." Her pleased grin was like the sun bursting out from the dark and heavy clouds that had been hanging over his head for so long.

He took another, longer drink. "I'm beginning to rethink the marriage question. Especially if I could start every day with this."

Which beat stopping by Starbucks on the way to work. Which had him thinking if Lani had been waiting at home with her French press, he may not have gotten run over on the way back from Tess's townhouse that night of her bomb threat.

"It seems more practical to send you back to Portland after New Year's Day with a grinder, a French press, and a bag of beans."

"You're right about the practicality. But the scenery's a helluva lot better here." Looking at her over the rim of the mug, his gaze moved over her tanned, bikini-clad body.

"I've always claimed Orchid Island is the prettiest of the Oceana group," she said, purposefully missing his meaning as she broke three eggs into a bright yellow bowl. "Why don't you take your shower while I make breakfast?"

A cold one, Donovan thought as he left the kitchen, headed toward the bathroom made for sex.

"I was going to replace your bathroom tile today," Lani announced when he returned to the kitchen. "But it's stuck in a bottleneck at the port in Honolulu. Hopefully it'll arrive tomorrow." She added cream cheese and smoked salmon to the eggs she'd poured into a pan.

"Did you ever reach your friend?" The woman hadn't answered her phone when Lani had called her from the Breslins' house.

"No. I called her again last night after I got home. And three times this morning." She shook her head. "But there wasn't any answer."

"Maybe she and that Ford guy eloped last night," he suggested. "And she was calling to tell you before they left the island."

"Perhaps," Lani murmured, clearly unconvinced as she snipped fresh chives into the mix. "But you'd think she'd at least answer her phone."

"Probably not if they're on their honeymoon."

"I suppose that's a point. But I can't believe she wouldn't have called me first. Ford runs a charter boat. I thought it would be fun if we could all have a twilight dinner sail this evening, but if she doesn't call back, I guess that's off the table. Meanwhile, we're taking you shopping."

"I am not, under any circumstances, going to wear one of those damned flowered shirts."

Lani sighed and reminded herself to be patient. He was, after all, *a malihini*—a newcomer—and should be allowed time to adjust. "May I remind you that my dad wore one last night? And that I thought he looked great?"

"It fit him," Donovan agreed. "He's not only a native, he's the king of the island. Literally. Which means he can pretty much wear whatever the hell he likes."

"Point taken. But you can't deny that Tom Selleck looked hot in them in Magnum P.I."

"Selleck is an actor. He was playing a part. The shirts were part of his character's laid-back image."

"But not part of yours," she guessed.

Just when she thought he might be beginning to unwind, he reverted to the man who'd shown up here yesterday. "Lani, I'm a police detective. My image is supposed to be a symbol of authority."

Lani decided that this was not the time to point out that she'd never been all that fond of authority figures.

"All right." She took the pan off the range and tipped the folded omelet onto a plate. "I'll let you off the shirt hook for now, but those jeans have to go because they're heavy and bulky, and don't dry fast when they get wet. Which they will. The same as your shoes. Except for hiking over the lava on the volcano, you'll need slippahs." When she saw him about to argue, she clarified. "Otherwise known as flip-flops on the mainland."

"No. Period. Way."

"They're more than an island fashion statement. They're practical because they dry fast and it's easy to shake the sand off them."

"I don't remember any fashion police when I was down here with Nate."

"Maybe not. But I'll bet you ended up borrowing his stuff."

His brow furrowed as he thought back. "Yeah. I guess I did."

"See?" She flashed him her best smile. The same one she'd pulled out while contestant wrangling on *Beauty* in order to urge intimate sharing in the "confessional" segments.

"The thing is," Donovan argued, "I don't need to worry about getting wet or sand in my shoes today because I'd planned to sit out on the lanai and get some studying done."

"Wrong again," she answered cheerfully, ignoring his frown. "Since the library's not open today, and the tile hasn't arrived, as soon as you finish that omelet, we're going sightseeing. And, if you're very, very nice, before shopping, I'll even take you snorkeling and introduce you to Moby Dick."

"Since I had to wade through the damn book in freshman English, Moby Dick isn't really a draw."

"You'll like this one. He's an *uhu*, or parrotfish I feed every day." She nodded at the untouched plate sitting in front of him. "And if we keep arguing, we're going to be late, and believe me, it's no fun being scolded by a fish."

"You're telling me you've befriended a fish named Moby Dick. Who talks."

"Would I make something like that up?"

"I'm not sure. Especially after you led me to believe your father considers Horatio your brother."

"My bad," she said cheerfully.

He shook his head and scooped up a bit of the omelet. "I don't know which one of us is crazier—you for talking to a fish, or me for agreeing to tag along to watch you do it."

Lani had only a split second to decide whether to be annoyed or amused by his aggrieved tone. She opted for amusement.

"Don't knock it," she said with a jaunty grin, "until you've tried it. You know, Donovan, it certainly wouldn't hurt if you allowed yourself a little fantasy now and then."

She took his mug, intending to put it in the dishwasher when Donovan snagged her wrist. "What makes you think I don't allow myself any fantasies?"

His voice was low and smoky, and his eyes, as they locked onto hers were like a tempest-tossed sea. Slowly, deliberately, even as those nagging little body parts that had been too long ignored began doing the tango, Lani forced herself to relax.

"I was simply teasing, Donovan. Gracious, must you take everything so seriously?"

"I'm a serious person, Lani. I always have been."

The fact that he had said it so simply, without apology, had her stifling her sigh. It also had her wanting to ruffle dark hair still damp from his shower and tell him to lighten up. Maybe they should tangle those sheets sooner rather than later. Surely morning sex would loosen him up.

With a fingertip, she traced his smoothly shaven jawline, breathing in the wood and sandalwood scent of the soap she'd bought at Natural Indulgences Soap and Candleworks next door to Taylor's Sugar Shack.

"I'll bet you were a Boy Scout."

"Eagle."

She smiled at that. "Why am I not surprised?"

"I wouldn't think anything could ever surprise you." Proving that he could, indeed, surprise her, Donovan stroked the inside of her wrist and caused a jolt in her pulse.

How could what should have been a casual touch make her tremble? Because, Lani realized, for Donovan, there were no casual touches. No simple conversations. Everything the

man did, what he said, was serious and seemingly meticu-
lously planned.

Would he be so controlled in bed? No. From the phero-
mones jolting back and forth between them like lightning
bolts, she'd bet her new titanium diver's watch with electronic depth meter that Donovan was a sex god. After all, so
much pent up energy had to go somewhere.

Lani grieved for the young man she had not appreciated
when they'd first met: the rookie patrolman who had acted
on his instincts. Instincts that were undeniably dangerous,
perhaps even a bit foolish. That young man probably would
not have risen through the ranks as far as the one now sitting
with her in Nate's sunny kitchen. But she doubted he'd have
that aura of sadness hovering over him like a heavy Oregon
fog.

She could make him happy. That was what she did. Her
true talent, like her father's bedside manner, her mother's art,
Nate's writing. Hadn't her baby-chick contestants assured
her it was her calling? Which was, of course, why she'd had
no choice but to leave them.

Right now, even as part of her wanted to strip off her
clothes and lie beneath him, hot, sweaty, and naked, while
he did anything and everything to her needy, tingling body,
an equally strong part of Lani wanted to put her arms around
him, put that beautiful dark head on her breast, and assure
him that he deserved better than the life he seemed to have
made for himself back on the mainland. That she could make
things better. That he could have that life with her right here
on Orchid Island.

And wasn't that a dangerous, impossible fantasy?

Oh, Nate, she thought with an inward sigh. *Even if I had been wanting to fall in love, you couldn't have sent me a more unlikely candidate.*

"You've surprised me, Donovan," she admitted quietly. She'd never been one to hide her thoughts. Not even when it cost her a lucrative and satisfying career. "More than I would have thought possible."

Instead of looking pleased by her admission, Donovan frowned. "Lani—"

"We're losing the day," she said with forced brightness as she pulled away. Nothing about Donovan Quinn was going to be easy. Then again, was there anything really worth having that was? "Come on, Detective. I'm going to get you to unwind if it's the last thing I do."

The hell with Nate and the hell with island time, Donovan decided. Lani Breslin was no longer Nate's petulant underage sister. She was, as he'd informed her brother, an adult woman.

An adult, deliciously scantily clad woman he wanted with every awakened atom in his body.

He ran a slow, insinuating hand up her bare thigh. Hadn't she told him to go with his impulses? "I can think of better ways to relax than running around playing tourist all day."

She backed away so quickly you'd think she'd been zapped by one of his unstable, electrically charged breakaway atoms. "There you go again, city man. Rushing things." She patted his cheek. "Didn't anyone ever tell you that anticipation is half the fun? Unless you're up for skinny-dipping, go put some swim trunks on beneath those jeans, because you're going snorkeling."

Knowing determination when he saw it, Donovan did as instructed and returned to where she was waiting in the great room.

"Well?" she asked over her shoulder when he hesitated for a glance at the abandoned laptop sitting on the table. "Are you coming or not?"

Apparently, he considered, as he followed her out the door, not any time soon.

6

"**S**UGAR IS ONE of Orchid Island's major industries," Lani said as she steered the fire-engine-red Jeep through the forest of tasseled sugarcane.

For all her talk of the pleasures of life in the slow lane, Donovan estimated that she was going at least sixty miles an hour down the pitted dirt road.

She shifted gears and pressed down on the accelerator, passing an enormous truck loaded with freshly cut sugarcane on the right. Donovan resisted the impulse to close his eyes.

"Actually," she said, waving gaily at the truck driver she was fast leaving behind in a cloud of dust, "sugar's so dependable that it's almost a religion on the island."

"I thought you said that things move more slowly down here," he said as the sugar cane became a blur.

"Time," she corrected. "I don't remember discussing driving."

"Do you think we could take this tour at a pace somewhat less than the speed of sound?"

She looked somewhat surprised by his ironic tone, but eased up on the accelerator. "That's the Sleeping Lady." She pointed toward a rock formation that did indeed resemble a reclining woman. "Kekepania was a giant *akua*, or goddess, who befriended the Menehune.

"Little people," she explained at his questioning look. "They were here even before the first Polynesians arrived. They were two feet tall and did all their work at night. They also had magical powers."

"I suppose you believe in them," Donovan responded, venturing a guess.

Lani turned her head to give him a knowing grin. "I like to," she admitted, "although there are those horribly unromantic souls who persist in believing that the Menehune were actually a class of pygmy laborers from Tahiti."

"You have to admit it makes more sense than the idea of pixies."

Apparently Lani was not prepared to concede any such point. "To some. Those with limited imaginations. However, while historians and anthropologists continue to argue about the Menehune, no one has come up with a logical explanation for all the stone water projects that were supposedly built by them in a single night.

"Anyway," she continued, "one night Kekepania was asleep when enemy canoes were threatening to beach on the shoreline. The Menehune threw boulders onto her to wake her up so she could come and protect them, but she was snoring and swallowed some of the boulders and died."

"That's too bad."

"Isn't it?" she agreed on a sigh. "Still, a few rocks ricocheted off her breasts and sank the invaders' canoes, so it all worked out in the end, I suppose."

She belonged here, Donovan determined. In fact, he had never met an individual more suited to her environment.

Cinderella, Sleeping Beauty, King Arthur, all would feel at home in this fantasy land of nature and legend. Donovan was having difficulty picturing Lani living anywhere else.

"That's Moon Cove Beach," she said, waving her right hand in the direction of a quiet stretch of sand they were passing. "The water's calm there; it's ideal for swimming."

She downshifted, slowing the Jeep to allow Donovan a leisurely look at the glistening beach. "Because it's so old, Mother Nature has more time to create our gorgeous beaches.

"Shipwreck Beach is great for windsurfing, Nalu Beach and Makani Beach are good for bodysurfing, windsurfing, and catamaran rides. Makalapua Beach is also where you'll find a lot of swimmers, Crescent Beach is good for surfing—"

"I get the point," he broke in. "And it's nice of you to play tour guide, Lani, but I don't really think I'll have time for surfing and catamaran rides. I do have—"

"Work to do," she said, cutting him off, just as he had interrupted her.

Donovan thought he detected the hint of an accusation in her dry tone. "Studying," he corrected. "I have an exam coming up when I get back that scores twenty-five percent on the written, and seventy-five percent for the interview."

"Both of which I have no doubt you'll ace," she assured him.

"That's probably what most of the would-be agents who made it through the first part of the acceptance process thought, despite knowing the odds. Which can be as low as one percent of the applicants."

"If you're serious about becoming a special agent, you'll make the grade."

"I appreciate your confidence, but I need to study. I bought these guides." All, on their online sales pages, promising success in winning one of the toughest, most prestigious jobs in the world.

"If all you plan to do is keep your nose stuck in a book, why did you come down here?" she asked, genuinely curious. "Surely you could have studied in Portland."

"Of course I could have. But Nate and Tess convinced me a change would be helpful."

"A change of location? Or pace?"

"Is there a difference?"

As they continued down the highway, the scenic bay curved out toward the backdrop of mountains. Rainwater scored the lush green mountain face in rivulets of molten silver. Donovan tried to remember when he had seen anything so magnificent.

"It depends," Lani answered at length. "If you lock yourself away in Nate's beach house and do nothing but pore over those study guides, you might as well have stayed home. A change in location isn't going to make any difference.

"However, if you forget about work for a while and open yourself up to everything the island has to offer, then I'd say you did the right thing coming here. Because even if you do go through with the test, you'll undoubtedly score better if you're not so tense."

"I'm not that tense."

"Liar," she said without heat.

He wasn't going to get into an argument he couldn't win. Since she was right and they both knew it. "What, exactly, does the island have to offer?"

"The best way to find that out," she said, decelerating as she suddenly turned off the main highway, "is to take things one day at a time and leave yourself open to surprises."

Donovan wondered if Lani realized that she was the most unsettling surprise he'd had in years. In a lifetime, he amended, casting a quick, sidelong glance at her profile.

The short road cut through the lush, fragrant greenery, ending at a tall white lighthouse.

"Lanikohua Lighthouse," Lani announced in her tour-guide voice as she brought the Jeep to a sudden stop with a screech of brakes. "Standing on the northernmost point of the island, it serves as a beacon to ships and planes en route to and from Asia. It also claims the second largest clamshell lens in existence, right after the one on Kaua'i. These days it's fully automated, but as you'll see, the view is spectacular."

"It is certainly that," Donovan agreed, his eyes on Lani as she jumped out of the Jeep. The shirt fell midway to her thighs, drawing his attention again to those smooth, golden-tanned legs.

The urge to touch her again was suddenly overwhelming. Donovan reached out and brushed his thumb along her cheekbone. "All these years that he's extolled your many virtues, Nate forgot to mention what a beautiful woman you grew up to become."

"You know how brothers are," she said lightly "Nate undoubtedly still thinks of me as having red braids down to my waist—which he yanked more times than I'd care to count, by the way—a hot temper, and a mouth full of railroad tracks." Taking his hand, she led him to the edge of the bluff. "Check this out, Detective."

Multihued blue water swirled dizzyingly far below them, breaking on the rocks in sprays of frothy white sea foam. Lani was standing on a rock beside him, her eyes bright with exhilaration.

"Isn't it glorious?" she asked breathlessly, throwing back her head to gaze out over the water, which reflected every color of blue from shimmering turquoise to deep indigo and all the shades in between. "Whenever I come here, I have an almost uncontrollable urge to fling open my arms and fly off into the sky." Her lips curved into a wide smile. "Some kids dream of digging to China. I always wanted to fly there."

Her cheeks were flushed a deep apricot and her hair was blowing free in the warm breeze, like a gilt-and-copper halo. She looked every bit as carefree, as welcoming, as the native Orchid Island women must have looked, standing on this very bluff, watching Captain Cook's ships sail up the coast.

No wonder that long-ago Breslin mutineer from New Bedford, Massachusetts, had fallen in love with the island, Donovan mused. Lani Breslin was part fantasy, part flesh-and-blood female. And he wanted both more than he could remember wanting anything in his life.

He was struck by a sudden urge to capture the breathtakingly sight of her. So that years from now, when he was chasing down terrorists, worrying about rising crime statistics, or whatever other sleep-stealing problems the future might bring, he could look at the photograph and remember what total freedom looked like.

"Really, Donovan," Lani complained lightly when she heard the unmistakable click of a cell phone camera. "If I'd known you were in the market for a model, I would have brought along one of my father's."

"I don't want one of your father's models. I want you."

His meaning was clear. There was a hint of annoyance in his tone that Lani opted to ignore. After all, from what she could tell, he'd tamped down his emotions so tightly for so long, awakening them would have to be initially uncomfortable for him.

"We need to get back on the highway. I still have a lot to show you."

Donovan ran his fingers down the back of her neck. "What about the smiles you collect along the way being more important than the miles covered?"

In spite of her heart pounding like a tribal tiki drum, she managed a smile at the familiar saying. "You're catching on, Detective Quinn. There may just be hope for you yet."

"I certainly hope so," he murmured huskily as he leaned down to kiss her.

His lips were firm, yet rather than demanding a response, they coaxed silkily, enticing her into the slow, but definitely serious kiss.

The breeze cooling her uplifted face was tinged with the crisp, tangy scent of the sea, and the sun felt warm, blissfully so, against her eyelids. Below, Lani could hear the crash of the surf as it beat endlessly against the rocks, and somewhere in the distance a seabird called out as it scanned the surging tide for silvery fish.

The reality of place and time gradually ebbed, like sands being washed away beneath a retreating wave.

When her mouth opened in a soft sigh of acceptance and wonder, Donovan thrust his tongue between her lips, drawing forth a moan. As the kiss deepened and her body melded against his, he felt as if they were standing on the very edge of a furious volcano. Flames tore at his restraint. Heat, fire, and smoke surrounded them, threatening to sweep them into the fiery core.

Slowly, gradually, Donovan became aware of yet another sensation. "It's raining again." He was surprised the soft, cooling water against his heated skin didn't create steam.

"Liquid sunshine," she corrected against his mouth. "Oh, more," she demanded, pressing her lips against his with renewed strength.

His body was still on fire, molten lust surging through his loins, and Donovan knew that they were reaching the point of no return.

"Lani," he warned, "we have to stop."

"Why?" Her lips on his throat had his blood pounding like surf in a hurricane.

"Because we're out in the open, in public, on the edge of a cliff, but in another minute, I'm going to forget all the reasons this is a bad idea."

"Don't you ever give in to impulse?"

His answering laugh was rough and raw. "Sweetheart, what do you think I've been doing ever since I got here on the island?"

His frank response broke the sensual mood. She tossed up her chin. "I have a name, Donovan. And if you're going to consider me some dangerous threat to your control, I'd prefer you use it, rather than a less-than-flattering generic 'sweetheart.'"

Hell. Could he have handled this any worse? "I'm sorry. It's just that I didn't come here for a vacation fling. I'm here supposedly deciding what I'm going to do with my life and where I'm going."

"And where you might have gone wrong?" she asked. Apparently not one to hold a grudge, she rubbed at the spot between his brows where the headache that had been threatening had hit like a damn missile.

"Now you sound like your brother."

He was exactly where he had set out to be so many years ago when he'd first climbed into that patrol car. When he'd determined to prove his famed neurosurgeon father and equally renowned psychiatrist mother wrong when he'd chosen a career in law enforcement over medicine.

"And except for the drive out here, we haven't exactly gone slowly."

"True enough." She let out a slight sigh. "Appearances to the contrary, I don't believe in being reckless. But sometimes, in some situations, there's a lot to be said for following your impulses. It's like being up here on the very edge of this cliff and looking down into the water. If you allow yourself to think about it, you'd turn around and climb right back down again. But sometimes, you just have to close your eyes and dive in."

His brows drew together. "And what if you land in dangerous waters?"

"That's the risk you take, I suppose."

He half smiled. "You make it sound so easy."

"And you make it sound so difficult." Shrugging off the impasse for now, she linked her fingers with his. "We'd better get going or we'll hear an earful from Moby Dick for being late."

7

TENSION HUMMED BETWEEN them like an electrical wire downed in a hurricane as Lani pointed out different scenic attractions while they drove along the coast. From time to time, she'd sneak a glance at him, finding the granite set of his jaw less than encouraging.

Men, she mused exasperatedly. They were so damnably sensitive—why did women bother to put up with them at all? As soon as Lani had asked herself that rhetorical question, the memory of Donovan's kisses provided the definitive answer.

Lani wanted him. On the beach. In her bed. Or better yet, beneath that outdoor rain shower she'd installed.

Wherever she could get him.

"Here we are," she said as she pulled the Jeep off the road several minutes later. "Just as a matter of idle curiosity, are you going to sulk all day?"

"Men don't sulk."

"Oh, that's right. Your kind merely broods manfully." She ran her fingers over the top of the steering wheel. Then sighed. "This situation isn't easy for me, either, Donovan. And we *are* going to have to deal with it. But, at the moment,

I need to call Taylor again, and Moby Dick is waiting for his breakfast."

• • •

THE PRISTINE WATER, intricately laced with a network of coral formations, was teeming with marine life of all kinds. Sea grass waved serenely in the slight current while brilliantly colored and patterned fish dashed among the branches of coral like tropical birds flitting through the delicate limbs of stony trees.

Vivid pink and red sea anemones expanded like soft and brilliant flowers, their sinuous tentacles waving enticingly as they lured unsuspecting victims into their embrace. Black-banded triggerfish approached Donovan curiously, searching for handouts, while a conspicuously striped orange-and-blue clownfish nestled safely among the stinging tentacles of a cluster of anemones.

A spiny lobster, looking like a giant insect, approached along the sandy bottom, armored legs lifted as if prepared for battle.

Lani tapped him on the shoulder, interrupting his fanci-ful thoughts, as she pointed across the silent lagoon. Cruising toward them and ignoring the other fish with regal dignity was a large turquoise fish with bright purple and yellow markings. Schools of smaller fish obediently parted like a silver curtain as the parrotfish swam in an unwavering line toward Lani. In this underwater world, he was undeniably king.

Lani reached into a small bag, taking out a yellow high-impact plastic waterproof camera, which she handed to

Donovan with a smile. Her eyes laughed behind the snorkeling mask she'd donned as the fish nudged her insistently. Impatiently. While Donovan snapped away on the digital camera, the parrotfish plucked frozen green peas from Lani's outstretched hand with comical but precise bucktoothed jaws, never once grazing her skin.

When Lani pointed toward Donovan, appearing to introduce man and fish, Moby Dick's shiny black eyes seemed to meet his in an almost human, oddly somber gaze. Then he blinked, giving Donovan the strange impression that perhaps, just maybe, something had registered on both sides. Before Donovan could dwell on the meaning of their silent exchange, a school of long-nose fish swam between them like a sunburst, shattering the fanciful interlude. Shaking his head bemusedly, he followed her as she swam back toward the beach.

"Well," she demanded, pushing her mask up onto her forehead as they stood in the knee-deep water, "now you've met Moby Dick."

Donovan took off his own mask. "He didn't talk to me."

Lani shrugged. "Didn't I mention he uses telepathy?" Her teasing gaze turned suddenly serious. "What did you really think?"

He reached out, pushing back some clinging strands of wet hair from her face. "I think," he answered slowly, "that this morning will go down as one of the most overwhelmingly beautiful experiences of my life. Thank you for it."

"We were only snorkeling, Donovan, something I do nearly every day. It's really not all that profound."

He pondered that for a moment. "Perhaps not profound," he agreed, "but vastly enjoyable. There was something almost otherworldly about it."

Even as she experienced a rush of pleasure at his words, Lani was distressed by the fact that he had echoed her own thoughts so clearly. She'd been trying to remind herself of all the things she and Donovan Quinn did not have in common. All those reasons that whatever happened between them could never be anything but an enjoyable vacation fling.

The idea that they could share feelings other than sexual attraction would make things even more difficult.

"You don't take much time out for enjoyment, do you, Donovan?" she asked, forcing herself to focus once again on the differences between them.

"I've been known to play a hole or two of golf."

"With the mayor and the police commissioner," she guessed as she retrieved a thigh-length cover-up emblazoned with a brilliant silk-screened rainbow from the backseat of the Jeep and pulled it over her head. "I'll bet you've never gotten through a game without discussing your work. You know your lowest score on every course you've ever played, and unless you at least match it every time out, you spend the remainder of the day irritated by your performance."

"There you go again, with that imagination." Rather than admit how close she'd come to guessing the truth, he took out his phone and shot another photo. "And speaking of imaginations, I just thought of a wish."

"A wish?"

Following his wicked gaze, Lani glanced down at her chest. "Oh. That doesn't count; it has to be a real rainbow."

"Since when are you such a stickler for rules?"

Her grin was quick and filled with sunshine, denying the mist that had started falling from the single cloud in the blindingly blue sky. "Since I had to start dealing with you."

She tossed him his clothing. "Get dressed, Donovan. I'm taking you to lunch."

•••

FIVE MINUTES LATER, Donovan found himself seated at a tapa-topped lacquered table, facing a wall of glass that provided a panoramic view of Mahini bay.

When Lani had first led him past the tiki poles draped in sparkling red, yellow, and green Christmas lights that marked the entrance to the elegant restaurant, Donovan had been struck by a sudden urge to put on a tie, despite the fact that every man in the place was wearing shorts, flip-flops, and either a T-shirt or aloha shirt.

"Still suffering from culture shock?" Lani asked sympathetically as she stirred her drink. A small paper parasol adorned the top of the red plastic swizzle stick.

"Is it that obvious?"

Lani observed him judiciously across the four-top as she took a sip of rum punch. "Only when you keep trying to straighten your tie."

"At least I'm providing some amusement."

"Don't be so sensitive. I think it's kind of cute." She speared a plump shrimp with a pair of bamboo chopsticks.

"I'm not sensitive." He took a pull on his bottle of Bikini Blonde Lager.

"You could have fooled me. And when did they pass a law in Portland outlawing police detectives to have a sense of humor?"

"Are you aware of the fact that every time you refer to my occupation, you heap an extra helping of sarcasm on it?"

"Now who's got an overworked imagination?" she asked mildly.

"You're ducking the question. What do you have against my work?"

"You're taking an innocent comment far too personally, Donovan."

"No, I don't think I am."

Her frustrated sigh ruffled her bangs. "For heaven's sake, it's not that I've actually got anything specific against your work—"

"You have no idea how that relieves my mind," he drawled.

"Do you want me to answer your question or not?"

He shrugged. "I'm probably going to regret this, but go ahead."

"I don't think you're happy."

"Okay. Hell. You've got me. I confess, since your brother will probably tell you anyway if you ask him." He held up his hands. "I'm burned out, drifting, the department shrink diagnosed me as midline depressed, so Nate and Tess sent me down here to unwind. Are you happy now?"

"Of course I'm not happy to hear that you're troubled." She braced her elbows on the table, linking her fingers together. "Sightseeing and snorkeling's a start. But I'm not sure it's enough to cure a serious case of burnout."

"Did I say it was serious? I've been through some stuff lately, and needed a break. So, here I am. And no offense, Lani, I'm not sure you're in a position to diagnose a case of occupational burnout," he said. "You appear to have created a life that suits you. And that's great. But despite all those degrees, you're not exactly the most hard-driving person I've ever met."

"No offense taken," she said mildly. "And I didn't think you'd listen." She leaned back in her chair, crossing her legs in in a smooth movement that Donovan couldn't help noticing despite his discomfort. Her eyes met his across the table. "Can you honestly tell me that you enjoy your work?"

"If it was supposed to be fun, they probably wouldn't call it work."

"Where have I heard that before?" she murmured. Then shrugged, shifting her gaze to the magical vista of the bay and the lush green mountains ablaze with flowers. "I can remember when you loved being a policeman," she said quietly.

"You were so busy complaining about everything and everyone around you that Christmas that I hadn't realized you'd noticed."

She treated him to an enigmatic smile. "Oh, I noticed, all right. Thinking back on it, I've come to the conclusion that part of the reason I behaved so abominably toward you was because of the way you made me feel things I was too young to understand."

Another surprise, he thought. "And now?"

"I understand them all too well," she said with a light laugh that faded as she treated him to a longer considering look. "But getting back to the topic at hand, doesn't it get tiring?"

He leaned closer, idly playing with a lock of her hair. "Doesn't what get tiring?"

"Always having to maintain a facade of being totally in control. Of continually being the man in charge."

Donovan shrugged. "It comes with the territory. I've gotten used to it."

Of course he had, Lani realized. She'd spent last night after she'd returned to her cottage, Googling him. From what she read, his image was that of a paradoxical man who could be charming, intelligent, dogged, and ruthless.

"It's also gotten you a lot of media coverage."

"I'm not going to apologize for using the media, Lani. I always considered news coverage the best way to telegraph the message to the bad guys that society will not accept their actions. Perhaps some of them will think twice before committing a crime. And if they don't, then they'll be dealing with me."

Lani recalled one interview she'd viewed on YouTube last night. The cool toughness Donovan Quinn had projected when announcing how a joint FBI/Portland Police Bureau task force had cracked a Pacific Coast ring raking in billions in illegal profits by selling arms and aircraft to enemy governments had certainly dispelled any idea that organized crime was untouchable.

"You may have a point," she said softly, watching the red sails of a small boat flutter in the wind. "And I totally get why the FBI wants you. I also realize that it would be a definite feather in your cap, and I've not a single doubt that you'd be terrific at keeping the world safe from terrorism. But is the FBI what you really want?"

"Of course it is," he insisted. "I've worked hard for this, Lani. I deserve it. And I want it."

If he seemed to be protesting a bit too much, Lani decided not to remark on it. "I don't know what's come over me lately," she said with an apologetic smile. "I'm not usually so judgmental. It must be the full moon."

"The full moon was last week."

"Blame it on the waning moon, then. Or the tides. Did you know that seventy percent of the human body is water and that the very same percentage of water makes up the earth's surface? How can we not be affected by things like tides?"

Her eyes were too bright, her tone too brittle. Donovan had made the false assumption that she was one of those blissful souls who drifted through life, like those fish they'd swum among earlier, without a care in the world. He'd assumed wrong. Again.

"How indeed?" he responded, deciding a public restaurant wasn't the best place to discuss what was obviously a personal topic.

Something was affecting both of them. And Donovan knew damned well that the tension that arose between them without warning and with increasing frequency could not be attributed to moons or tides or any other such fanciful notion.

Even as she kept checking her phone for calls or texts, as if by mutual consent, they turned the conversation to lighter, less controversial topics—the weather, recent films, whether Portland or Orchid Island could boast the best seafood restaurants.

They were lingering over coffee when a tall, stunning blonde, clad in a pair of red shorts and a red-and-white candy-cane-striped top came rushing up to their table and sat down in one of the empty chairs. "I'm so glad I found you!" she said breathlessly.

"I've been trying to reach you since last night," Lani said. "I want you to meet Donovan Quinn, Nate's best friend from the mainland. Donovan, this is Taylor Young."

"It's nice to meet you, Taylor," Donovan said, extending his hand.

"Hi." The woman's eyes barely skimmed over Donovan as she ignored his outstretched hand. "Lani, I have to talk to you. *Now.*"

Despite the fact that Taylor was head over heels in love with Ford, Lani had never seen her friend so upset that she'd so pointedly ignore any male, especially one as good-looking as Donovan was, even with his weight loss, which she was determined to reverse.

"Sure. Why don't you join us for coffee?"

As Taylor's distressed eyes returned to Donovan, he got the message. Loud and clear. "I think I'll walk off some of that lunch on the beach," he said, tossing some bills onto the table. "Why don't you catch up with me later, Lani?"

Lani's grateful eyes thanked him silently as she nodded her agreement. Taylor appeared to have forgotten his existence.

He'd seen that look before, Donovan mused as he walked along the edge of the wet sand. More times than he cared to count. Taylor Young was a stunning woman—when she wasn't scared out of her wits.

Hell. He'd been a cop too long. It was probably just some female thing like a problem deciding on which wedding dress to buy. Or the fiancé wanting a chocolate cake while she wanted white.

Even as Donovan told himself that, he couldn't quite make himself believe it. And Lani's solemn expression, as she walked toward him twenty minutes later, only corroborated his gut instinct that there was a great deal more to her friend's problem than mere wedding plans.

"Ford's gone," She said as they returned up the beach to where she'd parked the Jeep. The mist that wasn't quite rain had stopped, and the fresh air was softened with the scent of flowers.

"He bailed on the wedding?"

She shook her head. "No, I mean he's disappeared. Ford and Taylor both own their own businesses. Taylor's candy store is the Sugar Shack and Ford runs a scuba shop, Pacific Paradise Adventures next door. When he didn't come back two days ago from a charter to Maui, Taylor thought he must've picked up another job."

"Sounds reasonable, given that you've already pointed out things like clocks and schedules aren't as rigid down here. And it would make sense, if he had a chance to pick up some extra bucks to put away for a honeymoon, he'd jump at it."

"That was what Taylor thought. And I agree that it's feasible. As for him not answering his phone, cell signals can be sketchy even on land here. On water, farther away from the towers, it's even worse."

Even as she seconded her friend's assumption, Lani's eyes were filled with worry. During his years as a cop, he'd seen that look before. Usually right before things went to hell. "But he's still not back," he guessed, knowing the answer.

"No. Taylor's afraid that he's in some kind of trouble. She spent all last night looking for him. That's why I couldn't reach her."

"Maybe the original clients decided to extend their trip," he suggested. "Or, like you said, he took on another charter."

"But Ford wouldn't have just taken off like that without a word. He'd have known Taylor would be worried sick."

"There's always another explanation. Maybe he changed his mind about getting married."

"I've known Ford since he first arrived on the island nine months ago. He adores Taylor. He wouldn't run out on her. And if he did have misgivings, which I don't believe he did, they would have talked them out. The two of them share *everything*."

Once again her words sounded so very familiar. Donovan wondered vaguely how many distressed women he'd seen come into the station, certain that something terrible had happened to their husband, lover, fiancé, significant other, partner. Ninety-nine percent of the time, the guy had just gotten his fill of domestic life and split. Of course, there was always that one percent....

"Has she gone to the police?"

"Yes." Lani made a sound of sheer disgust. "Not that our local police are going to win any medals for investigative techniques. They believe that he's left her."

"It happens, Lani," Donovan said quietly. "Even in paradise."

Jerking her hand from his, Lani twisted the key in the ignition. "Not with Taylor and Ford," she insisted firmly as she turned the Jeep back toward the highway.

A moment later, she shot him a speculative, sideways glance. He could practically see the wheels turning inside that gorgeous red head.

"Donovan, I have the most marvelous idea."

"No."

"You don't even know what I'm going to say," she complained.

"You're going to suggest that since the police refuse to look for Taylor's missing fiancé, I check into it."

She gave him a warm, persuasive smile. "I know you could do it, Donovan. Don't forget I was in Oregon when you went into that warehouse and captured the armed robber. I thought you were the bravest, most amazing man I'd ever met."

"You sure as hell could've fooled me," he grumbled, remembering how he'd returned home from the ER that night flushed with success. Lani's sulky indifference had quickly burst his little bubble of self-congratulation.

"Surely you're not going to hold my foolish teenage behavior against me?"

"Of course I'm not. But that doesn't mean that I'm going to go off on any wild-goose chase for your friend's missing scuba diver, either."

"But you *are* a detective."

"I'm also supposed to be on vacation, as you keep pointing out."

Lani glanced over at him, undeterred by the grim line of his jaw. "Surely it wouldn't take that long—"

"Lani," he warned in a low, serious voice.

"All right," she said as she returned her attention to the winding road. "But I don't know how I'm going to tell poor Taylor you refused to investigate Ford's disappearance."

"You already volunteered me, didn't you?"

"Oh, look," she said brightly, dodging the question. "Coming up on your right is Makalapua Beach, which I told you about. You'll probably recognize it because Hollywood shoots South Seas scenes there all the time. Many people consider it the prettiest beach in all of the islands. Of course other people argue that Hanalei, on Kaua'i, where Mitzi Gaynor washed that man right out of her hair in the movie *South Pacific,* is the best because it's famous. But this is my favorite."

"That's very interesting. And I'm sure it's a great beach. Even the best beach in all the Pacific. But at the moment I'm more interested in what you told your friend."

"Honestly, Donovan," Lani complained, "you really do need to learn to relax."

A moment later, Donovan was treated to a scene that lived up to its hype. The velvet-green mountain and golden coral sand, fringed by pandanus trees, was separated from the vast blue Pacific by a long ruffle of dazzling foam. The vista evoked all the mystical beauty of the South Seas. It also served to reduce his exasperation. Somewhat.

"Paradise found," he murmured.

Lani gave him a distinctly wary but appreciative glance. "Isn't it?"

She pulled off the road and cut the engine. Draping her wrists over the top of the steering wheel, she gazed out over the sun-brightened sea.

"Sometimes, when I'm feeling down, I'll come up here and just sit on the beach, watching the waves. Before long, I'll believe in the magic again."

Donovan slipped his arm loosely over the back of her seat. "That's important to you, isn't it? The magic?"

He could hear her soft, rippling sigh. "This will probably only reconfirm your feeling that I'm crazy. But I do believe in the magic. Sometimes it's the only thing that keeps me centered during difficult times."

Her solemnly spoken words cut through to some hidden core. Donovan hadn't expected such a serious answer to what had been an idle question.

He studied her profile carefully, unwillingly intrigued by this new aspect of Nate's sister. As far as he had been able to tell, Lani lived the carefree existence of a tropical nymph. What could she possibly know about hardship? Yet the note of pain he detected in her soft voice suggested hidden depths she wasn't yet prepared to share.

"Are you still mad at me?" she asked. "I know I was wrong to tell Taylor that you'd help her find Ford, but she was so upset, and Nate's always telling me that you're the smartest detective on the West Coast, so when the idea popped into my head, I just blurted it out."

Her expression was so earnest that Donovan couldn't resist a smile. "I suppose I could talk to her," he agreed reluctantly.

"That's very nice of you, Donovan. Remind me to reward you for this display of gallantry."

He leaned across the console, and, with a finger, lifted her chin. "I have every intention of doing exactly that..."

Slowly, deliberately, he closed the gap between them, bent his head, and took her mouth. Their lips touched once. Briefly. Lightly. Then again. And again.

He certainly didn't kiss like a man suffering from burn-out, Lani thought as sunshine seemed to flow through her veins. Taking her hand, which had somehow lifted to his shoulder, he pressed it against his chest. While her heart was beating like a rabbit's, his heartbeat was strong and hard. Just like the rest of him.

"If this is the reward I get for agreeing to talk to your friend, I can't wait for the payoff when I find the guy," he said, touching his lips to her temple.

Lani closed her eyes briefly, luxuriating in the feel of his lips against her skin. "Then you do believe that something's happened to him? That he hasn't really jilted Taylor?"

"I believe Taylor believes that," Donovan hedged.

"But you don't." Before he could respond, Lani drew apart and held up the hand that had been exploring his chest beneath the T-shirt. "Please don't answer that until after you've talked with her and heard the story firsthand."

"I suppose that's next on the agenda?" Although he knew he was playing with fire, Donovan could think of a great many more pleasurable ways to spend an afternoon with Lani. Beginning with washing off the salt water from snorkeling beneath that outdoor rain shower Nate had had her put in.

"No, Taylor has to go to Honolulu tonight—something about a mix-up with the company that supplies her chocolate, which is really important because she's got a big order to ship out to California—so you're meeting her tomorrow morning for breakfast."

"For someone so upset, it seems she's got her priorities a little reversed." In his line of work, that was definitely a red flag.

"She's already gone to the police," Lani said, the lack of conviction in her voice revealing she shared his misgivings, but wasn't prepared to admit it. "And got them to notify the Coast Guard to watch out for his boat. But she also has an interview to appear on *Shark Tank,* so it's vital that the order go out on time and sell well so she'll impress the investors enough to make a deal that will allow her to continue to expand her company off the island."

"I imagine appearing on that program is quite a coup."

"There's a lot of competition," she agreed.

"I don't suppose you had anything to do with her beating the contestant odds."

"I may have made a few calls," she said, with a vague wag of her hand. "I do still have friends in the business. But I wouldn't have contacted them solely for friendship. Her chocolate really is that good. Wait until you taste her Macadamia dark chocolate truffles. They're to die for."

From Lani's description, and the brief meeting, Taylor Young didn't sound like the type of black widow who ended up on all those court television shows on trial for murdering a lover, fiancé, or husband. But the situation, which wasn't yet a case, had Donovan's spidey senses tingling. Still, FBI study books aside, he was supposed to be here on vacation, this wasn't his jurisdiction, it would probably turn out to be nothing, and the idea of an evening alone with Lani trumped talking to a bride-to-be who appeared more concerned about growing her business than finding her missing fiancé.

"While you were walking on the beach, I got a text from my grandmother," Lani said. "She's sorry she missed dinner last night and wants to see you."

He glanced down at his rain-rumpled clothing. "I'm not sure I'm properly dressed to visit island royalty."

He'd learned the story of how a Breslin woman several generations back had married a distant cousin of the former queen of Hawai'i. Which, since Orchid Island had managed to remain independent of the other islands during their civil war, essentially made Lani and Nate's father the king of Orchid Island and Lani's grandmother the queen mother.

Lani glanced over at him. "No problem." She turned the key to start the Jeep's engine. "We can stop on the way."

8

A FTER A STOP at the island clothing store, which involved
a great deal of compromise (mostly on Donovan's part,
he felt), he left wearing a dark blue polo shirt with a magenta
tribal design across his chest, khaki board shorts, and mesh
canvas Vans. Having finally been declared suitably attired,
ten minutes later he was following Lani through a winding
maze of overgrown hibiscus bushes toward a house that was
an oddly eclectic mishmash of architectural styles.

Although he'd met Lani and Nate's grandmother when
he'd originally visited several years ago, he'd never been to
her home. Constructed of red brick, it might have been New
England in feeling had there not been huge white marble col-
umns out front, and a wide porch, which gave it an antebellum
air. A series of Victorian cupolas rose from a Spanish tile roof.
It was as if the house had changed hands several times in the
construction process, each new owner adding his own imprint,
rather than scrapping previous plans and starting fresh.

They were led into a screened solarium, filled to abun-
dance with tropical plants. The atmosphere in the room was
humid enough, Donovan was certain, to grow mushrooms
through the bleached plank flooring. His head was swimming

with the sweet scent of the vivid hothouse flowers when his attention was drawn past a towering banana plant to a ninety-something woman seated regally in a bamboo peacock throne chair.

Despite the sweltering heat, she was bundled in a shawl of soft wool. Antique gold rings adorned every finger, and the woman's wispy hair, which had once been an almost blue-black, was now a bright shade of purple, contrasting with her pink scalp into a pastel tapestry.

The entire scene evoked some long-past era. However, the vast assortment of electronic equipment—state-of-the-art cameras, night vision goggles, satellite dishes, high-powered telescopes, a computer console that looked capable of launching nuclear weapons, and two drones sitting on a counter—could have come straight from the Department of Homeland Security.

"I don't think I'm in Kansas any longer," Donovan murmured.

"Speak up, young man." The woman's voice rang out.

"I was just commenting on your equipment."

"Isn't it nice? I used to have to order from Spy Store catalogs. Now, thanks to the Internet, I can keep up to date with whatever's new on the market."

The woman's eyes turned to Lani. "It's about time you brought a man home," she said, holding out her arms.

Lani knelt beside the chair, giving the woman a hug as she pressed a light kiss against her weathered cheek. "You know I always do what you tell me to, Tutu," she said, using the Hawai'ian word for grandmother.

Margaret Breslin snorted. "Ha. If only that were true. You're like your brother. Both of you have minds of your own." The old woman's gaze returned to Donovan. "You're that policeman friend of Nate's. It's good to see you again. Even if you are too skinny."

"We're working on that," Lani said.

"I should hope so. You should do something about that limp, as well." She turned her attention back to Donovan. "I slipped and hurt my hip a few months ago. Lani has the most amazing massage that will fix you right up."

"I'm sorry about your hip," Donovan said.

"So was I. More because it was such a damn stereotypical old lady thing to do. If it weren't for Lani, I'd probably be stuck in that wheelchair the doctor tried to keep me in.

"Nate told us all about your adventures when he was here with his darling Tess for Thanksgiving," she said, segueing into a different topic. "I'm not at all surprised you're looking overworked. A terrible thing, what happened to Tess. And gracious, I can't imagine what it must have been like for those poor people in the Pacific Northwest living with that serial killer among them. I'd never leave my house."

"You barely do now," Lani murmured beneath her breath, but Donovan heard it just the same.

"Is that new?" Lani asked. In an obvious attempt to change the topic, she pointed toward a black-and-chrome entertainment center that looked as though it could have come from the bridge of the Starship Enterprise.

"It just arrived yesterday," the elderly woman confirmed with a broad smile. "This little baby just happens to be cable equipped for 380 channels. And surround sound. It also has editing capability for video."

Her laugh was rich and delighted as she rubbed her beringed hands together. "Old Sturm und Drang will die from envy when he sees this." Her sparkling eyes laughed up at the thirty-something man standing beside her, who thus far had remained silent. "Won't he, Kai?"

"We'll hear the explosion from here," he answered with a nod of his dark head.

"Sturm und Drang is Tutu's nickname for Maximilian Heinrich von Schiller," Lani explained in answer to Donovan's questioning glance. "He was one of her early directors. In fact, Max took credit for launching her to stardom."

Despite her advanced years, Lani's grandmother proved her hearing was still that of a young girl by overhearing Lani's murmured explanation.

"Which is ludicrous!" she spat out, banging an intricately carved cane imperiously on the floor. "If anything, it was *I* who saved *Max* from drowning in that trashy stew he was making of *Island Girl*."

Even before Donovan had met Margaret Breslin, he'd known about her, having watched two of her movies in a college film class. Her star had taken off like a blazing comet when she'd appeared on the screen swimming supposedly nude in a lagoon not that different from the one he was staying on.

Given that the studios found it far easier to jump on a bandwagon than build one, her next movie, *The Sailor and the Island Girl*, a mild, innocuous romance by today's standards, between a marooned sailor and the curvaceous, scantily dressed Polynesian girl who'd found him unconscious on her beach and hidden him from enemy soldiers, put her in the pantheon of actresses who became known as sex goddesses.

Margaret's voluptuous curves, clad in a clinging silk flowered sarong, had even appeared as a Pinup Girl on the nose of a World War II bomber. Exuding sex appeal from every pore, she'd proven the perfect fantasy girl for GIs who'd lived day-to-day, never knowing if it would be their last. She'd also worked tirelessly for war bond drives and had accompanied Bob Hope on a tour of the South Pacific Islands racking up thousands of often dangerous miles entertaining the troops.

After the war, Sam Goldwyn signed her to MGM, casting her in World War II dramas, where she'd usually play a sarong-wearing island girl. She'd also appeared in a western where she'd been cast as a scantily clad Native American who'd tempted a cavalry officer, only to end up dying by a soldier's bullet during the inevitable battle. Then, finally, in the early fifties, she'd appeared in a rash of musicals and sudsy "women's dramas" in an attempt to stem the tide of moviegoers who'd begun turning to TV.

While the movie studios never regained the entertainment monopoly they'd once held, Margaret had continued to fill theaters, causing the movie mogul to tell famed Hollywood gossip maven Hedda Hopper, that "When Margaret Breslin waves her curvaceous hips in a Technicolor film, the box office instantly doubles."

Margaret had continued to work into the early sixties, when movies became more realistic, darker, and gritty. And the actresses, with their no-makeup looks and long, unstyled hair, looked a lot more like the girl next door than the too-hot-to-handle femme fatale a guy might dream of living next door. Savvy enough to quit before casting directors no longer came calling, she'd retired, becoming more reclusive as she grew older.

"I'll bet you're surprised I'm still alive," Margaret added with the forthrightness usually attributed to either the very young or the very elderly.

"Of course not," Donovan responded on cue, as he slipped the purple orchid lei he'd bought at a roadside stand around her neck and bent to brush his lips against each of the former actress's weathered cheeks. "Nate says you're still as strong as a Thoroughbred."

"And I'll bet he adds that I'm also still as stubborn as a mule," she said on a husky laugh as she touched her finger to one of those cheeks as if to savor the light kiss. "Now here you are, face-to-face with this very silly old woman who observes the world through a satellite dish and telescope."

"I thought Donovan would enjoy seeing you again," Lani cut in before he could respond.

Donovan thought it was interesting that Lani did not mention her belief that he'd been sent here to seduce her. She certainly hadn't had any qualms about telling her parents.

Margaret gave her granddaughter a very knowing look, pausing just long enough for dramatic effect. She was still quite an actress, Donovan reflected with appreciation for the outlandish scene Margaret Breslin had cast them all in. Of course, when you considered the other members of the Breslin family, the elderly woman seemed merely entertainingly eccentric.

"You've always been a terrible liar, young lady," Margaret retorted. "That's not what your mother told me during our morning call. Besides, I didn't just fall off the pineapple truck, you know."

She waved her hand dismissively as Lani opened her mouth to protest. "However, since neither of you seem prepared to make an announcement quite yet, we'll overlook the matter. For now."

"Grandmother, you are incorrigible." Lani's tone was firm, but a smile teased at the corners of her mouth as she sat down in a cane chair, its cushion covered with a colorful parrot print.

"I certainly hope so, my dear," Margaret agreed. "It's just about the only fun left to an old lady. Speaking of aging, my mind must be going soft: I haven't offered your young man refreshments. Which reminds me that I've also failed to introduce Kai, who's in charge of my Island Girl Organic Tea. Donovan, this is Kai Fletcher, whose family coincidentally dates back to that same group of whaling mutineers as ours. Kai, this is Donovan Quinn, a friend of Nate's."

"Kai has his Ph.D. from the University of Hawai'i in tropical plants and soil sciences," Lani volunteered.

"Nate told me his grandmother had hired someone to take over a failing tea plantation," Donovan said to Kai. "It's nice to meet you."

Donovan also knew the story of a dozen mutineers who'd abandoned ship in order to get medical help for the ship's cook, who'd been badly beaten by an overly abusive captain. Once the whalers had been welcomed warmly to the island, they'd refused to return to the ship and had become farmers, storekeepers, and traders who subsequently supplied other whaling ships.

"You, too. Nate claims you're the Steve Jobs of tea," Donovan told Kai.

Kai laughed at that description. "Nate's a writer. He enjoys hyperbole. In reality, tea plants were first brought to the islands in the 1800s. But Asian tea pretty much had a monopoly on the market, and since pineapple and sugar-cane proved more profitable, farmers developed those crops instead.

"It wasn't until the 1980s that a new generation of farmers re-explored the idea of commercial tea farming with help from the local USDA office and the university. More recently, as people became more interested in eating local, a few of us formed a collective to share what we learn. To farm tea, you need acidic soil, good drainage, a higher elevation—"

"Island Girl Organic Tea Farm is at four thousand feet on the side of Mt. Waipanukai," Margaret broke in.

"The rain forest at that elevation provides a steady seventy-five to ninety percent humidity," Kai explained. "We also have steady sixty-to-eighty degree temperatures, which creates a sweeter tea and ample sunlight. Also, being grown on volcanic soil, our leaves take on a distinct flavor that stands out because of its brighter, clearer flavor profile...

"Let me get you a cup and you can taste for yourself."

"Thank you," Margaret said. "And please bring us some of that coconut pie. We're going to put some meat on this boy's bones before we send him back to the mainland." The elderly woman peered at Donovan with bright, inquisitive eyes. "I've heard Lani's feeble explanation. Now why don't you tell me the real reason you've come to the island."

"Nate sent me here as a Christmas present for Lani," Donovan answered easily as he sat down on a matching chair next to Lani's. "I'm supposed to seduce her."

"It's about time someone did." The still-bright button eyes swept over Lani, subjecting her granddaughter to a long, studied appraisal. "Given that Lent has long passed...My grandson always did have exquisite taste in gifts," Margaret acknowledged, echoing Thomas Breslin's words of the previous evening. "I may just forgive him for not visiting me more often."

"Donovan is only kidding, Tutu," Lani insisted. "Tell her that you're joking," she demanded, shooting him a stern look.

Donovan enjoyed seeing her flustered. The soft pink color infusing her cheeks was decidedly attractive, and her sea green eyes flashed with passion that he'd already discovered.

"I'm not certain I am," he drawled, stretching his legs out in front of him as he subjected Lani to a slow, leisurely inspection. "Actually, the more I think about it, the more I find the idea vastly appealing."

As she was drawn into his dancing, deep blue eyes, Lani was forced to wonder, yet again, where she had ever gotten the idea that this man was harmless. Despite the stiff, formal clothes he'd shown up in, and what appeared to be a rigid amount of self-discipline, she suddenly had the feeling that he could be every bit as unmanageable as her grandmother and her parents. Or her brother. No wonder Nate and this man had been best friends for so many years.

As he watched the slow recognition dawn in her eyes, he flashed those dimples in a satisfied male grin.

Margaret's interested gaze did not miss the exchange between Lani and Donovan. "I like this one," she announced. "He knows how to add zest to the chase." Her ebony eyes sparkled up at Donovan. "There was a time when I would have enjoyed fighting that age-old battle of the sexes with you, Donovan Quinn."

He leaned forward, taking her creased hand and raising it to his smiling lips. "Believe me, Ms. Breslin, if you'd honored me with your interest, we wouldn't have wasted our time fighting."

As Margaret giggled like a schoolgirl, Lani didn't know whose behavior astounded her more—Donovan's or her grandmother's. Whichever, she had no more time to dwell on it as Kai returned with a tea tray, distracting Margaret's attention once again.

"Thank you, Kai. Everything looks lovely, as usual." She turned toward Lani and Donovan as the young man poured the steaming, fragrant brew.

"I brought you both black and green for a true sampling," he said as he put two cups in front of Donovan, along with a thick slab of coconut cream pie. Which, although Donovan wasn't a dessert guy, looked damn delicious. "Try the green first, because it's the lightest. Then move on to the black."

"Nobody brews tea like this man," Margaret said. "Tea leaves are very delicate. Only a master brewer knows precisely how much pressure to apply in order to waken the full flavor without damaging the surface. Bruised leaves give tea a bitter taste. Isn't that correct, Kai?" she asked brightly.

"They do," he agreed. "Though that isn't a problem with Island Girl, which is grown and hand picked to taste nearly the same if a buyer prefers tea bags for a shortcut."

Donovan watched as the woman sipped her tea with the air of a wine connoisseur sampling a vintage cabernet sauvignon. "Excellent, as usual," she proclaimed finally. "I can't wait until we get our tasting house built and gardens planted at the site. Not only will it be a good island tourism attraction, I love educating people about tea."

"You appear to know a great deal about it," Donovan said to Margaret.

"I do indeed, thanks to Kai, who's not only a brilliant grower, but a patient teacher. Of course, I did drink a lot of tea while playing the great Kublai Khan's wife in *The Romantic Adventures of Marco Polo.*"

"I saw that movie just last month," Donovan surprised both women by saying.

Lani slanted him a look that, though one of gratitude, told him he needn't bother to lie. Donovan steadfastly ignored her.

"You were the best thing in it," he continued. "I especially liked that part where you got down on your knees and begged your husband not to kill Marco Polo. Were those real tears?"

Margaret bobbed her head. "Of course. I never resorted to using fake tears. The studios might have cast me as a sex goddess, but I was always an actor at heart. Why, there was this one time…"

As interesting as she'd always found her grandmother's colorful tales, Lani's mind drifted as Margaret segued into a bit of juicy movie gossip about an off-screen affair between a hairdresser and the actor playing Marco Polo.

Lani was surprised by how instantly Donovan had taken to her eccentric grandmother. She had expected him to be polite, of course—she never would have submitted her beloved grandmother to deliberate rudeness. Reluctantly, Lani admitted that taking Donovan to her parents, and bringing him here today, were acts of self-protection.

She had wanted to establish boundaries, to prove to him that no matter how strong the physical attraction between them, they had absolutely nothing in common on which to ever base a long-term relationship.

Oil and water. That's what they were. Shake swiftly and they might come together for a short time, but that's all it could be. Yet, she allowed, it could be an amazing Christmas to remember...

Deciding that it was time to return home before her grandmother had her and Donovan engaged, Lani replaced her teacup on the gold-rimmed saucer with more force than necessary. Both Donovan and Margaret turned toward her.

"We should be getting back," she said in answer to Donovan's questioning look.

"You're the tour guide," Donovan allowed. Then turned to Kai. "Since I put myself through school working the Portland docks, I've always gotten my caffeine fix from coffee."

Hell, he'd take the stuff through an IV if he could. "But you may have converted me. I like the citrusy taste of the green, but the black's amazing." It was a deep mahogany color that had a faint taste of caramel and something else Donovan couldn't identify.

"The leaves are infused with dried cherry smoke while drying. It takes time, and we'll never be able to scale it enough for mainland wholesalers to stock it, but we're proud of what we've created here."

"You should be." He stood up and turned toward Margaret. "Thank you for your hospitality, Ms. Breslin," he said, taking her hand. "It's been a pleasure."

"Will you come back?" Her eyes betrayed a hint of pleading.

"I will." Donovan brushed his lips, old-style, against the back of her veined hand. "If you promise more stories. And tea. And the pie was delicious."

She nodded happily as she fingered the lavender orchid flowers of the lei he'd brought her. "I knew you'd like the tea, and my daughter-in-law made the pie. She'll be making more for the Christmas luau. Can I expect to see you there?"

"I'm looking forward to it," Donovan said. And realized it was true. When the topic had come up during the dinner, the only draw had been Lani. Now he realized he was looking forward to all the promised festivities. And spending more time with Lani's family, who was the polar opposite of his own.

"You've a real fan in there, Kai," he said as the tea planter accompanied them back through the floral maze to the Jeep.

"It's mutual. How many entrepreneurs do you know who'd start a new business at her age? Especially when it takes three years before you can harvest plants grown from seed. Which she insisted on doing."

"Tutu's a firm believer that people die when they stop having new projects to keep them interested and alive," Lani said.

"Thus the tea house and garden ideas," Kai said. "We're at blueprint time for the house now, and she's interviewing landscape architects, so there's no way she's going to run out of challenges anytime soon."

"She's a doll, and I adore her and admire her energy, but Tutu does bounce back and forth between the past and future sometimes without warning. Maximilian Heinrich von Schiller, by the way, passed on twenty years ago. Fortunately, Kai has amazing patience."

Kai shrugged. "I like her. A lot. Plus, I get my own house on the plantation and a salary that's way more generous than I could've gotten if I'd taken the offers to teach at the university or that job growing tea for Starbucks. I've been doing some pretty heavy investing and should be able to retire before I'm forty. Not that I'd want to. But since there's a lot of down time in the tea business, I also get time off for surfing. Thanks to your grandmother, my life is pretty freaking perfect."

• • •

LANI WAS QUIET as they drove back to the cottage. To Donovan's surprise, she drove at less than the speed of light and seemed thoughtful. Not wanting to intrude on whatever was going through that bright and busy mind, he remained silent, content to watch the scenery.

It was incredible, he mused, now able to understand her belief in magic. Jagged mountains sloped down to gorgeous bays through valleys carpeted with sugarcane and pineapple and dappled by shafts of reflected sunlight. The narrow winding road curved through lazy, sun-drenched villages where placid Buddhas kept eternal watch in Oriental cemeteries. Wind and wave, rain and river had sculpted the tropical island into a kind of fairylike reality that was magical. Donovan almost found himself believing in the mystical powers of rainbows.

"Thank you," she said after a time.

The sky was turning saffron and purple as Donovan dragged his attention away from the brilliant sunset. "For what?"

"For being nice to my grandmother."

He shrugged off her appreciation. "She's easy to be nice to. I like her. Actually, now that you bring it up, Lani, I like your entire family. A lot."

That wasn't supposed to be how her test turned out, Lani thought with a sinking heart. He was supposed to be shocked by her family's individual and collective eccentricities. Appalled. He wasn't supposed to want anything further to do with her. This new Donovan Quinn, the future FBI special agent or possible Portland Chief of Police, was turning her entire plan upside down.

"You didn't have to lie about seeing her Marco Polo movie."

"I didn't."

She narrowed her eyes. "Give me a break here, Donovan. You may be able to fool an old lady but not me."

"It was shown at a film festival the Police Benevolent Association sponsored for charity," he answered amiably. "Your grandmother's reputation and talent contributed to a lot of beds for Portland's homeless."

"Oh. You'll have to tell her that at the luau. It'll be a great Christmas gift to know that her movies are not only remembered but helping others."

"I'll do that." He reached out, putting his hand lightly on her thigh. "So, what are the plans for the evening?"

"Evening?"

"Evening. You know, that quiet, romantic time after the sun goes down. When the world slows down to catch its breath. Evening," he repeated patiently.

She glanced over at him in surprise. "Since the twilight dinner sail is obviously out with Ford still being MIA, I hadn't made any other plans."

Donovan ruffled her hair in a carefree, affectionate gesture. "Don't worry," he said with a bold grin that reminded her of one of the pirates who once sailed these seas. "I'm sure if we put our heads together we can think of something."

Lani found the unexpected turn of events, not to mention his provocatively husky tone and the lambent flame gleaming in his deep blue eyes, far from comforting.

Strangely light-headed, she returned her attention to her driving, ignoring Donovan's deep, self-satisfied chuckle.

9

DONOVAN FELT HIS plans for a romantic evening for two disintegrate like fog under a bright Orchid Island sun when they approached the cottage and found Thomas Breslin waiting on the front lanai.

"Aha!" Thomas called out, waving his straw hat in welcome. "You're back. I was just getting ready to leave."

Donovan cursed his decision not to have Lani stop so he could take a picture of the neatly squared rice paddies and taro patches along the river they'd passed. From the vantage point afforded by the highway, the peaceful scene had reminded him remarkably of the Orient. If they'd only stopped for five minutes—three, even—he could have avoided what he knew was going to be a long evening listening to Lani's father wax philosophical about the arts.

"I brought the painting over in the SUV," Thomas said, lifting up a large, bulky package wrapped in brown paper and tied with string. His next words confirmed Donovan's worst fears. "As well as a portfolio of some of my favorite sketches. I thought as a fellow art aficionado, you'd undoubtedly enjoy an artist's view of the island."

Donovan ignored Lani's low chuckle. "I can't think of anything I'd enjoy more," he said weakly.

Lani patted his arm. "Have fun," she said cheerfully as she turned to head down the beach to her own cottage.

Unwilling to allow her to escape quite yet, Donovan wrapped his fingers around her wrist. "What would you say to my dropping by for dinner after your father leaves?"

They were moving too fast. She needed time to think. Time to figure out what she was going to do with this man. "Sorry," she said with far more aplomb than she was feeling, "I'm going to bed early. I have to work tomorrow."

"Putting in my tile?" He found the idea of Lani puttering around the cottage all day extremely pleasing.

"No, the library's open tomorrow and it's children's reading day, so I'm working. And you have to get up early to have breakfast with Taylor."

"Where?"

"Pronto Lanai on Kapoli Bay. I'll have Kenny Palomalo deliver a GPS equipped car with first thing in the morning because you're going to be needing your own transportation while you're here."

"I didn't think there was a rental car agency on the island." Which had resulted in his less-than-satisfactory cab experience.

"There isn't an official one because, unlike the other islands, we're not that into becoming a crowded, hectic tourism destination." She flashed a quick grin. "Call us selfish, but we prefer to keep our beaches to ourselves. But Kenny's a car dealer who rents used cars and trade-ins on the side to the occasional tourist who does show up. Or someone who needs a loaner."

"What time?" he asked resignedly, suspecting the meeting was going to be nothing but a waste of time. Even if the missing fiancé hadn't returned home, he'd listen to Lani's friend's story, then, after assuring her that she was undoubtedly too good a woman for the guy, he'd be on his way. Although those study books were calling, maybe he'd drop by the library to take Lani to lunch. Better yet, a picnic on what he was already beginning to think of as "their" beach.

"Ten," she said. "Call me after you talk to her?"

Ten was early? Not wanting to get into yet another discussion about differences in time and life-styles, Donovan merely nodded. "Sure."

She smiled up at him. "Thank you. It's very nice of you to jump in like this when you have important things of your own to do."

"Nothing as important as you." Which had become the truth. "Thanks for the tour."

"Don't mention it. Orchid Island may have broken away from Hawai'i during the first King Kamehameha's wars to unite the islands, but far be it from me to give you the idea that we Orchid Islanders aren't overflowing with the aloha spirit."

For not the first time since meeting Lani, Donovan felt unreasonably powerless as she turned on her heel and began jogging down the expanse of sand.

"She's more complex than she appears at first glance," Thomas offered as he came up beside Donovan. "People look at Lani and fall in love with the free spirit, never guessing there's an intelligent, flesh-and-blood woman living inside that attractive packaging."

Donovan didn't feel it prudent to tell Thomas Breslin that what he was feeling for the man's daughter was a great deal more basic than love.

"She's got a lot of her grandmother in her," he murmured instead.

Thomas looked at him with renewed interest. "So she took you to visit Margaret, did she? Last time you were here, you only met her in passing, when she arrived at the house just as you and Nate were off to go surfing. What did you think?"

"I think that you must have had an extremely interesting childhood."

Thomas threw back his head and laughed heartily. "What a wonderfully circumspect answer," he said, throwing a friendly arm around Donovan's shoulder. "*Interesting*," he chortled. "That's one word for it."

They entered the cottage and were sipping white rum on ice when Lani's father turned the conversation away from a rundown of the island sights Donovan had been shown that day.

"I'm a bastard."

Donovan wasn't fooled for a moment by Thomas's casual tone. The gleam in those intelligent eyes revealed that it was a test, and both men knew it.

"You shouldn't be so hard on yourself," Donovan drawled. "From what I've witnessed so far, you're an amiable enough man."

Thomas nodded, accepting the ball as it returned to his court. "That's what all my patients say," he acknowledged. "However, I was speaking in the biblical sense. My mother was never married to my father."

Donovan shrugged, unconcerned. "So?"

"It ruffled more than a few feathers back in those days. It doesn't bother you?"

"Not a bit," Donovan answered honestly. "Does it bother you?"

"Of course not," Thomas answered impatiently. "But as you've already pointed out, my childhood was not exactly the norm. My mother's circle of friends could be described as bohemian at best and more than one of my surrogate relatives was blacklisted during the McCarthy era. Including my birth father."

Donovan thought he knew where this was going. He put the glass down on a rattan table beside the chair. Leaning back, he rested his elbows on the arms of the chair and linked his fingers together.

"We're not really discussing your parentage here, are we?"

Appearing uncharacteristically uncomfortable, Thomas Breslin tossed back the rum. When he returned his gaze to Donovan, he was no longer smiling.

Donovan had seen that same expression on Lani's face from time to time. Secrets, he mused. The Breslin family definitely had its share.

"She's my daughter, Donovan. And I love her."

"Of course you do."

Thomas stared down at his empty glass, as if wishing it could magically be refilled. Then he lifted his head to give Donovan a warning look. "I don't want her hurt," he said with a low forcefulness that was at direct odds with the cheery, carefree character he'd seemed last night.

"What makes you think I'd do anything to hurt her?"

"You wouldn't mean to," Thomas allowed. "I can tell you're a decent man, and Nate's always spoken highly of you. But you're going to. I can see it coming, and damned if I know how to stop it."

"I have no intention of hurting her. Yet, as I've already told Nate, she's a grown woman. She's also smart, self-aware, and capable of making her own decisions."

"That's true. But there's no future for you and my daughter. How likely do you think the FBI would be to hire a special agent whose wife's father testified before the House Un-American Activities Committee?"

"Are you asking me my intentions?"

"No. I'm asking you not to use my daughter as a diversion," Thomas responded with a burst of heat. "Something to while away a tropical holiday before you return to Oregon and move on with your life."

"I don't want to argue with you, Thomas, but our relationship really isn't any of your concern."

The older man dragged his hand wearily over his face. "I didn't think it would work," he muttered as he rose and made his way to the door.

"Then why did you bother to make the attempt?"

He turned in the doorway, looking as if he had suddenly aged a lifetime. "She's my child," he said simply. "I love her."

With that he was gone, taking his portfolio but leaving the wrapped painting. Donovan stood in the doorway, watching until Lani's father was out of sight. Then, pulling out his phone, he called the mainland.

10

NATE PLOWED HIS hand through his hair as the phone across the room rang. Having been working on the same chapter for the past two days, the last thing he needed was a damn interruption. Leaving the caller to get sent to messaging, Nate continued to stare doggedly out over the windswept cliffs of Sunset Point, demanding his muse to come through and help him out of the corner he had managed to write himself into.

The phone chimed again. And again. Finally, going over to scoop it up, he recognized the number and swiped it open.

"I hope you realize that you're interrupting a literary genius at work."

"That's nothing compared to what you've done to me," Donovan complained on a gritty tone. "I thought you sent me down here to relax."

"That was the idea," Nate agreed.

"So how the hell am I supposed to relax when I'm surrounded by your crazy family?"

"They're getting to you, huh?" Nate asked with a low chuckle. "Which ones?"

"Which ones?" Donovan repeated. "Name one who isn't. I take that back," he said after a fleeting moment's consideration. "Your mother, so far, has been grace personified. However, it wouldn't surprise me in the least if she dropped in at any minute with some lightly veiled warning to keep my roaming hands off your sister."

"She'd call first. She may be an artist, but my mother could give Miss Manners a lesson when it comes to social protocol." He paused to fill in some features on Tess, who he was absently sketching.

"Regarding my sister, have your hands been roaming since we talked this morning?"

"Like I told your father, who warned me away from her in no uncertain terms, that's none of your business."

"I thought it was strange when he called me a while ago," Nate said. "Dad usually stays out of our personal lives. So what did you do to get my usually easygoing father so uptight?"

"Nothing yet." Donovan's voice was sharp with obvious frustration.

"Aha. The plot thickens. I assume Lani's receptive to whatever you've been up to?" Nate added some fullness to Tess's upper lip. Although his writing paid for his Victorian cliff-side home, Nate enjoyed sketching. His father had always claimed credit for that particular talent, and Nate had never thought it necessary to correct him.

"Are you asking as a friend? Or Lani's brother?"

"That's a rough one. A friend," he decided. "I've already given you my big-brother spiel."

"I think she does. Correction, I know she does. But every time I think I have her figured out, she throws me a curve."

"We all have issues. She might come off like some fairy sprite at times, but that doesn't mean she's any different. Give her time," Nate advised as he added an arch to Tess's brows before using the side of the pencil to draw in long dark waves that kissed his fiancée's cheekbones. "Get to know her. After all, you've only been on the island a couple days. Things move slower down there."

"So I've been told," Donovan muttered. As a detective, he was used to sifting through mountains of evidence for the single missing piece that would nail a bad guy. Since arriving on Orchid Island, he'd discovered an impatience he hadn't known he possessed.

"Then what's the problem?"

"Hell. To tell you the truth, I've no damn idea why I called."

Impulse, Donovan decided. He'd done the first thing that came to mind after Thomas had left. But that was totally out of character. Not only had he developed a respected reputation for thinking before he acted, he'd never been one to discuss his personal life with anyone, even his best friend.

He and Nate regularly discussed careers, politics, the state of the world, and sports. But they had never, in his memory, had a conversation concerning either of their dealings with a woman. Not a specific one, at any rate. Not even about Tess, whom he'd casually dated before she'd fallen in love with his best friend.

He'd assumed that she'd told Nate that nothing had ever happened between them. He'd certainly never brought the topic up, and neither had Nate. So, what the hell was Lani doing to his mind?

"Sorry about interrupting your work," he said, feeling like some love-struck teenager crushing on a cheerleader.

"Hey, no problem," Nate answered absently.

"Get back to work." Donovan recognized that tone. He'd just lost Lani's brother to whatever muse was whispering in his ear.

Nate's only response was a vague murmured agreement as he added a small, still unnoticeable baby bump. Although he'd wanted to shout the news of his impending fatherhood from the rooftop to the world, or at least to their friends and families, he'd agreed to respect Tess's desire to wait a few weeks before revealing her pregnancy.

He wondered what Donovan would say if he'd told him that he understood his problem, all too well. His writing had suffered while he'd been trying to not only convince Tess they were meant to be together but worrying about keeping her alive long enough for her to agree to marry him.

After yesterday's test strip had come up with a pink plus, he was finding it more and more difficult to live with a mind swirling with horror.

"You have a contract," he reminded himself as he returned his attention to the computer screen. "A deadline. Baby stuff to buy." Which, having married friends, he knew was a lot of stuff. The crazy thing was that he was actually looking forward to it, but he'd rather surrender his left nut than attend a baby shower. Which he wouldn't have to do, being a guy. Would he?

Putting that worry aside, he stuck on the noise-blocking earphones and was rewarded by the imagined sound of dogs baying eerily through a swirl of thick, icy Puget Sound fog.

He was back on track. Immensely gratified, after making a mental note to go online and order some of those books about what to do when you're expecting, he began tapping away at the keys, leaving his best friend to handle his own romantic dilemma.

•••

As the deserted beach caught the last moment of evening sun, Donovan Quinn opened one of the downloaded test books and went to work, determined to put Lani and her colorful but highly distracting family out of his mind.

He spent most of the night and the early part of the next morning poring over the sample interview questions. Unfortunately, his thoughts kept drifting around the corner to her beach house, and by the time Kenny Palomalo had delivered a decent, low-mileage Taurus with a full tank of gas and only minimal rusting and he left to meet with Lani's friend, Donovan couldn't remember a single thing he'd read.

The meeting, which took place over a diner breakfast of fried Spam, hash browns, and eggs, was uninformative and explained why the police chief hadn't been interested in her story. All the signs pointed to the conclusion that this Ford guy was nothing more than a douche with itchy feet.

Having spent eight years drifting around the South Pacific, the nine months Taylor Young's fiancé had spent on the island was the longest he'd settled anywhere. With marriage looming in the new year, he'd undoubtedly felt the noose of unwanted responsibility tightening around his neck and had taken off before he suddenly found himself buying furniture, making mortgage payments, and losing diving and surfing time to attending parent-teacher meetings and kids' soccer games.

On the surface, that's all the case amounted to: another woman growing a little wiser the hard way. But something had been nagging at the back of Donovan's mind since Taylor had first arrived at the restaurant thirty minutes late, with that vague, obviously concocted reason for having been on Oʻahu he hadn't bought when Lani had told him about it. She did not, he noted, name the so-called chocolate supplier she'd supposedly been meeting with.

After insisting that her fiancé wouldn't have jilted her, she gave him a recent photograph of the guy and promised to let him know if she remembered anything he might have said that would shed some light on his disappearance. Outwardly, she was cooperative. She was also lying, Donovan concluded as he drove toward the library on the windward side of the island.

Over the years working for the Portland Police Bureau, he'd dealt with a great many liars, and he'd bet a month's salary that the lissome Taylor Young was another. That she was hiding something was obvious. But what? And why? He might have only agreed to talk to her for Lani, but damn if this case didn't have him unwillingly intrigued.

11

H E FOUND LANI seated in a green meadow, surrounded by a group of wide-eyed children. Her cotton sundress, emblazoned with brilliant orange and gold poppies, billowed about her, making the flowers appear to have sprung from the fragrant volcanic earth. A creamy hibiscus was tucked behind her ear. Donovan couldn't remember ever seeing anything so lovely.

"He was a very nasty giant,'" she read aloud to the avid young listeners, "forever sticking his tongue out at people and calling them names."

"Just like Johnny does," a young girl piped up.

"I do not," an obviously rankled boy, whom Donovan took to be the accused, shot back.

"Do, too."

"Do not!"

"You do," the girl repeated insistently.

"Hey," Lani broke in mildly, "I thought you wanted to hear the story." Her tone, though soft, carried the unmistakable ring of authority. The two combatants fell silent.

Lani nodded. "That's better," she said with a smile.

"There! He did it again," the girl called out, pointing a finger at Johnny as he stuck his tongue out at her.

"Johnny," Lani admonished sternly, "that's enough. If you and Debbie don't stop squabbling, you'll both have to go home without hearing the end of the story. Is that understood?"

Eyes downcast, two dark heads nodded obediently.

"Now, where were we?" Lani murmured.

"The giant was calling people bad names," a helpful listener offered.

Lani flashed the boy an appreciative grin. "Thank you, Paulo."

The color deepening the boy's already dark skin told Donovan that the dazzling smile was no less effective on six-year-old boys than it was on grown men.

"Anyway," Lani continued, "people were getting very tired of this nasty, ill- tempered old giant. Finally, another giant tossed the obnoxious fellow into the ocean where sharks ate every bit of him. Except his tongue. It was too bitter even for a shark to eat. They spit it back out and—"

"It turned into the black rock on Shipwreck Beach," someone broke in eagerly.

Lani rewarded her audience with a smile. "That's right."

"Read us another." The group took up the cry, young voices high and enthusiastic.

"Well, I suppose we have time for one more. Who wants to hear the legend of Kanunu?"

A flurry of hands shot up. All except one, who'd caught sight of Donovan.

"Who's that?" the little girl with sleek black hair and almond eyes inquired, pointing toward Donovan.

As she lifted her head, Lani's gaze met Donovan's steadily watchful one. Soft color bloomed in her cheeks. "I think," she said, "that we've read enough for today." The resultant complaints sounded like a Greek chorus of doomsayers, but one that Lani ignored.

"Nolina," she instructed the girl who'd first taken note of Donovan, "would you please tell Mrs. Yukimura that I'm going to take a short break and will be back in a little while?"

"Are you Lani's boyfriend?" the little girl asked, lingering behind the others to study Donovan with somber, unblinking eyes behind her round glasses.

Donovan smiled down at her. "I'm working on it."

"Mr. Quinn is my brother's best friend," Lani said decisively. "He's simply here for Christmas vacation. Now scoot. If you're a good girl, maybe Mrs. Yukimura will let you date-scan the books."

Apparently those were the magic words because the young girl took off like a shot, leaving Lani and Donovan alone.

"How was your breakfast with Taylor?" she asked.

"I ate Spam."

"That's no surprise. Given that it's the island's national meat product, thanks to all the GIs eating it during World War II. I was referring to what clues you came up with regarding Ford's disappearance."

"I'm still working on the clue thing. How long have you known Taylor Young?"

"We've been best friends since fourth grade. Why?"

"Do you know of any reason she'd lie about her boyfriend's vanishing act?"

"Lie?" She shook her head. "Taylor doesn't lie."

"She did this morning."

"I don't understand. Are you saying that she knows where Ford's gone?"

The warm sun was reflected in her hair, and unable to resist, Donovan walked over to her and ran his hand down the molten copper strands. "I'm not sure. But she does know a helluva lot more than she's telling."

"Why?"

He shrugged. "I've no idea."

"But you'll find out."

"I'll do my damndest. Not for her. But because you asked me to. Meanwhile there's something else I need to tell you...

"I thought of you, Lani," he said, getting to his real reason for having come here. Since he hadn't managed to get anything out of her friend, he could've called or texted her about the unsatisfactory breakfast meeting. "All night. And not just last night, but the night before that. I can't get you out of my mind."

"You certainly don't sound very happy about it." Nor was his frown at all encouraging.

"This can't go anywhere," he warned, as his hand slipped beneath her hair.

"And you call yourself a detective," she said as she decided that the touch of his fingers on her neck was the closest thing to foreplay she'd had in a very long while. And if he could have her bones melting with just that butterfly-light touch, what could he do to her body with that perfectly shaped mouth? "I figured that out between the lighthouse and the tea."

A long, vibrating moment hummed between them as he looked down at her, and Lani looked back up at him. Below them, the surf beat against the lava rocks crowding the narrow white beach, as it had for millions of years. The cry of seabirds, diving for fish, filled the plumeria-scented air, mingling with the carefree laughter of children frolicking in the playground adjacent to the small library building.

"Me, too. But that doesn't stop me from wanting you," he said.

"You're not alone in that. Me wanting you, I mean."

He shouldn't feel so good, she thought, looking out at the silver splash of a family of dolphins playing offshore while she gathered her scattered thoughts. Shouldn't taste so good. But he did, and heaven help her, she was so very, very tempted.

Lani was seriously considering taking the rest of the day off, when her phone chimed. "I'd better answer," she said, not taking her eyes from his. "In case it's Taylor."

He rolled his eyes, but nodded. "Go ahead."

It was. "Lani," the voice, edging near hysteria asked, "is Donovan with you?"

"As a matter of fact, he is."

"I need you," she said between sobs. "Both of you. Now."

"Of course." Donovan had dropped his hands and no longer looked anything like a man on vacation with seduction in mind, but rather the crime-busting detective he was. "Where are you?"

"At Ford's shop." More sobs. "Hurry!"

•••

THEY TOOK HER Jeep to the docks, where they found Taylor sitting in the midst of what could charitably be called a mess. It looked as if a hurricane had gone through Pacific Paradise Adventures.

Boxes of equipment had been slashed open and masks, snorkels, and tanks tossed carelessly aside. The usually well- stocked shelves were bare, their contents spread over the floor. A saltwater aquarium had been overturned; the gaily colored tropical fish lay lifeless among the wreckage. Ford's shop had been thoroughly, expertly ransacked.

"What on earth?" Lani stared in disbelief at the scene.

"It's no better next door," Taylor moaned, jerking her head in the direction of the door that connected the two businesses. "It'll take me all day to clean up all my candy-making supplies they threw out of the cupboards."

"What were they looking for, Taylor?" Donovan asked. From his calm expression, Lani got the impression that such vandalism was a routine event for him. All in a day's work. She marveled at his ability to remain composed when her own heart was beating like a jackhammer.

Taylor's blonde hair skimmed her shoulders as she shook her head. "I don't know."

"Dammit." Donovan crouched down in front of her, grabbed her shoulders, and gave her a firm shake. "Don't you realize this is getting serious? You could be in danger, Taylor. The goons who tore this place apart weren't just looking for something. They made this mess was to send you a message and Ford a message and could decide to come after you next. As soon as they figure out that you know what he's been up to."

Taylor's golden complexion went chalk white. "But I don't," she wailed. She turned accusing, tear-filled eyes toward Lani. "You didn't tell me he was so mean."

Lani shot Donovan a sharp look. "Can't you see she's had a terrible shock?" She joined them amid the rubble on the floor and took hold of her friend's hand. "Taylor," she coaxed softly, "why did you lie to Donovan?"

Taylor's startled green eyes flew to Donovan, seeking confirmation of Lani's words, but his expression remained inscrutable. "Oh, Lani," she said, "I wanted to tell you. But I was afraid you'd think that I'm a terrible person."

"Never," Lani assured her.

"A few weeks ago," Taylor said as she scrubbed at her wet cheeks with the backs of her hands, "a man came into my shop to buy some candy for his kids. He said he was an FBI agent who'd been sailing the islands and had dropped in for a meeting with the local police. Anyway, he was friendly enough, although a bit formal for my usual taste, and in a kind of stiff, mainland way, good-looking."

She glanced over at Donovan. "Actually, now that I think about it, he reminded me a great deal of you, Donovan."

"Thanks. I think," Donovan returned dryly. "What did this FBI agent want with you?"

"I told you," Taylor insisted, "he simply came into the shop to buy some saltwater taffy. But it was a slow day, and Ford had taken a two-day charter over to the Big Island, so I was grateful to have someone to talk to."

"What did you talk about?" Donovan asked.

"Really, Donovan," Taylor protested, "that's a little personal."

"In case you haven't noticed, this vandalism has gotten more than a little personal," Donovan pointed out. "So let's try it again. What did you two talk about?"

"Just the usual things men and women talk about when the man is trying to pick the woman up and the woman's trying to decide whether she's going to let him. Surely you've got a few tried-and-true lines of your own, Donovan."

She paused for a moment, waiting for a response that didn't come. Lani suspected that the long, drawn-out silence would work well during interrogations. It was certainly beginning to get on her nerves. And apparently Taylor's, as well, because her friend caved. As Donovan had obviously expected her to.

"After a while, he asked me if I wanted to have a drink with him," Taylor finally said. "Since I wasn't doing any business anyway, I agreed and closed the store early. Of course that was my big mistake."

"Why?" Lani asked.

"Because I was attracted to him, that's why. Despite the fact that he was all wrong for me. For heaven's sake, Lani, haven't you ever been irresistibly drawn to a man against your better judgment?"

As Lani felt Donovan's gaze shift to her, she refused to look at him. "Of course I have," she mumbled. "Are you telling me that things went beyond a drink?"

Taylor tugged her hand loose and began twisting it with the other in her lap. "Oh, I knew it was foolish. He told me up front he was married. And, of course, I was engaged to Ford. But after my third Painkiller—"

"That's not drugs," Lani jumped in to assure Donovan. "It's a drink. A very good one, actually, with dark rum, coconut, fruit juice with nutmeg on top. But it's lethal."

"Apparently." Donovan looked right into Taylor's eyes in a way Lani recognized. He had a way of doing that which she'd decided also was a result of his police work. "Go on."

"We went to his boat, which was docked at the marina, and had sex."

"Do you think perhaps Ford found out about it?" Lani asked. "And perhaps that's why he left the island?" *And you?* she thought but didn't want to say.

"I don't know," Taylor admitted. "We went to Da Conch bar instead of The Blue Parrot, where Ford always goes, which I thought would be safer, but it's possible someone saw us and told him."

"There's also a chance the guy who came into your store wasn't an agent at all," Donovan said. "Did you ask for identification?"

"No. But I didn't have to, because he flashed a badge."

"But you have a name."

"Bob."

"How about a last name?"

"I'm afraid not. He probably said it, but either I didn't catch it in the beginning or forgot after the Painkillers."

"I told you they were lethal," Lani said.

"Seems so."

Taylor Young's expression was miserable. And looked real enough. But then again, the Cascades Killer had looked as harmless as a choir boy. Which was how he'd avoided setting off internal alarms when he'd shown up at his victims' campsites claiming to be lost. And Ted Bundy hadn't coaxed all those girls into his VW by acting like the stone-cold serial killer he'd turned out to be.

"Well, with any luck, the police will have some ideas when they go over this place," he said.

Taylor paled visibly at his words. "Police?"

"You *are* going to call them, aren't you? They're bound to take the case more seriously now."

She paused for the space of a heartbeat. It was a struggle, but she managed to regain her composure. "Of course I'll call."

Hell. Donovan nodded brusquely. "Of course," he agreed, taking Lani's elbow and leading her out of the shop. "We'll check back later."

Once outside, Donovan pulled his shades from where he'd hooked them on the neck of his shirt and shoved them onto his face with more force than necessary. "For a woman supposedly unaccustomed to lying, your friend sure tells some whoppers," he muttered, the bridge of his nose aching as they returned to the Jeep.

"What does that mean?"

"It means that she no more hooked up with some special agent than I did."

Lani's eyes narrowed as she looked up at him. His gaze was frustratingly enigmatic behind the lenses of the dark glasses. "How on earth did you come to that conclusion? It was obvious that Taylor was horribly upset about what she'd done. For good reason."

"I'll give you that she's upset. And that she's got a good reason. But I'm not buying that story. It's nothing but a smoke screen to keep us from finding out the real reason for the vandalism."

"You can't know that for certain," Lani argued.

"Believe me, after a while you get a gut feeling that tells you when a person's being evasive, something your friend has been doing from the beginning."

"Whether you believe it or not, she's horribly upset about Ford's disappearance. And as much as I want to be with you, after what happened today, she shouldn't be alone at a time like this. I need to spend the night with her."

His face gave nothing away, but his eyes revealed both frustration and regret. "Not exactly what I'd had planned for tonight."

"Me, neither." So much for breaking her fast.

"Maybe this Ford guy will show up before tonight," Donovan said without conviction.

"Maybe." Anything was possible, right? And Mt. Waipanukai might erupt while they were standing there, his gaze moving over her face like a caress that promised the wait would be worth it. Wasn't she, after all, the one who'd been stressing the appeal of island time?

"Maybe she'll even tell you whatever it is she knows that she didn't want to share with me. I'll stop by the police station and have them do some drive-bys during the night."

Her blood, which had warmed nicely beneath his hot gaze, chilled. "Do you really think it's dangerous?"

"If I thought it was, I wouldn't be leaving you alone. But there's no point in not taking precautions. Meanwhile, I'm leaving for Oʻahu in the morning."

"Why?"

"In the beginning, I figured her fiancé just got cold feet," he admitted. "But I learned early on never to go for the easy answer. Now that someone has upped the stakes by vandalizing both shops, I'm going to do a little digging."

Lani's heart hitched. "Thank you, Donovan," she managed to say even as she realized that not only was she going to have sex with this man, she was now in danger of having her heart broken when he returned to his real life.

And your point is? that reckless heart and needy body asked.

Lani couldn't come up with a single answer.

He cupped her chin in the manly hand she was aching to feel everywhere on her body. "Don't think this little reprieve gets you off the hook," he warned. "A sexy, intelligent woman once suggested that I learn to follow my instincts. To act on my impulses. So, after giving the matter a great deal of study and consideration, I've decided to take her up on it."

This time her foolish heart didn't just hitch. It began turning somersaults as he bent his head and brushed his mouth against hers. "Do you have any idea how much I'm going to miss you while I'm off island?"

"I'm going to miss you, too." Which had to be the under-statement not just of the century, but the millennium.

"What would you say to forgetting about Taylor and Ford and spending the night making crazy mad love in your brother's passion pit?" When, apparently forgetting that they were on the street where anyone could see them, he plucked at her lower lip with his teeth, Lani's body spiked to to DEFCON Two.

"Don't tempt me," she managed on a weak moan as he pressed her against the driver's door of the Jeep.

"Why not? That's what you've been doing since you practically attacked me at the lighthouse."

"Me? Attack you?" She escaped that way-too-seductive touch and climbed into the Jeep. "You certainly have a selec-tive memory, Detective," she said as she fastened her seat belt.

"Okay, perhaps it was mutual," he said as he got in and fastened his own passenger seat belt. "But I certainly don't remember either one of us complaining."

She should know better than to try to argue with a man skilled in interrogation. "You're going to drive me crazy, Detective Quinn."

Donovan leaned across the console and planted a firm, noisy kiss on her tilted lips. "Count on it."

12

"SO WHAT'S THE story with the hot buns detective?" Taylor asked over takeout ham and pineapple pizza and wine.

"And here I thought you were going out of your mind with worry over Ford," Lani countered.

"I am. But that doesn't mean that I don't care about my best friend's love life."

"Donovan's only here on vacation. He'll be going back to the mainland after New Year's."

"That's what he says now. I've known more than one mainland type to get hooked on the islands. Look at Ford." With that, Taylor's eyes grew misty. "I'm so worried about him, Lani." Her expression was more earnest than Lani had ever seen it. "Your Donovan will be able to find him, won't he? He is as good as you say he is?"

"He's not *my* Donovan." As hard as she'd tried, Lani had not been able to get Donovan's allegations about Taylor out of her mind. "But Nate says he's the best. And he wouldn't be being considered by the FBI if he wasn't very good at his work."

She put her glass down on the table and leaned forward. "Taylor," Lani prompted gently, "have you told Donovan everything you know about Ford's disappearance?"

Something like desperation flashed in her friend's eyes but was gone before she could fully grasp its meaning. "Of course I did."

"Are you certain that you didn't leave something out? Something that perhaps slipped your mind at the time?"

"Really, Lani, I think you've been spending too much time with that detective. Since when do you cross-examine your best friend?"

"Maybe when she neglects to tell me she slept with another man. After asking me to be maid of honor at her wedding."

"I know it was wrong." Taylor's hands were shaking as she refilled her glass. "But Ford was spending more and more time away, which left me feeling lonely, ignored, and resentful. I was actually rethinking the whole marriage idea when Bob showed up out of the blue. And, well, like I said, things just got out of control." She took a long gulp of wine. "I swear, I'm staying away from rum from now on."

"There's another thing that occurred to me on the drive over here," Lani said, deciding not to point out that Taylor might have forsaken rum, but she was certainly making inroads on the wine. Another thing that was out of character. She'd always been a one-or-two glass drinker.

"What?"

"I was telling Donovan how the island has never really gotten into the tourism thing—"

"Ford wouldn't make a living without tourists from the other islands."

"True. But he's the exception."

"But not the only one who'd like to see more tourists," Taylor said. "Not everyone has relatives to leave them inheritances."

There was an edge to her friend's voice that Lani hadn't heard since she'd been packing to move away from the island. Looking back, she'd been going on too much about the new, exciting life opening up for her in California. It would have been only natural for Taylor to have felt resentful, and even abandoned, but she'd never said a negative word, had watched and texted about every episode *of Beauty Tames the Beast*, then welcomed Lani back with open arms and had even thrown a party for the occasion.

"I'm sorry if you have a problem with my family," she said, a bit stiffly. It wasn't as if the Breslins had done anything to become island royalty.

It had all begun when Lani's great-great-grandmother on her mother's side married a man who'd descended from the Kalākaua dynasty. Kalākaua was from Kaua'i and had ruled all of Hawai'i for a time. It had been his sister, Queen Liliuokalani, who'd been deposed by a pro-U.S. group who overthrew the kingdom.

Lani's great-great-grandfather had only been a distant cousin to the deposed queen, but being the only member left of the dynastic family on Orchid Island, he'd reluctantly accepted the crown after his father's death.

Previous generations had tried to get rid of the royalty, but islanders revered their past kings and queens nearly as much as they did their ancient gods and goddesses, and each time the referendum came up for a vote, the majority would vote to keep the status quo.

"I don't, really." Taylor sighed. "Especially since you floated me that loan to get the Sugar Shack going in the first place."

"We're BFFs," Lani said simply. "And it isn't like I did anything to earn the money." The inheritance, which admittedly allowed the family to indulge their interests without having to worry about paying the bills, had come from her great-grandmother. There would be more when Margaret passed. Which would be years and years from now, Lani assured herself.

"I know. And I sounded petty."

"No, you didn't. But would it make you feel better to know that I've been envious of you and Ford?"

"Seriously?" Far more interested in this conversational topic than Bob, the supposed FBI guy, Taylor topped off her glass. "Why? I didn't think you even liked Ford."

"All that matters is that you love him," Lani said, hedging her belief that the diver was a little too laid-back even for island standards. She'd known when she'd made the loan that part of it, maybe even all, would be going into his business, but wanting her friend's happiness, Lani had been happy to do whatever she could to help.

"Which is why I'm envious. My clock's ticking, my eggs are getting older by the minute, and you know I've always wanted a large family."

"I believe you settled on eight kids when we were in the fourth grade," Taylor remembered. "Then adjusted downward to five in high school."

"I'd settle for three now," Lani said. Then refilled her own glass for the first time. "Hell, who am I kidding? I'd take one. But it's hard to find a candidate on an island where I've known everyone all my life."

"Which is why I jumped on Ford when he sailed into the harbor," Taylor said. "He never knew me when I was chubby."

"You weren't chubby."

"Either your memory's shot, or you're just being extra kind because I'm fragile right now. That's only one of the words Madison Andrande and her clique of hangers-on called me in high school."

"They were mean girls," Lani reminded her. And still were from what she'd seen since returning home. Taking in Taylor's wet eyes, she hoped a crying jag wasn't on the horizon. "And how can you take anyone named for a New York City street seriously?"

"Good point." Taylor leaned over and planted a sloppy kiss on Lani's cheek. "So," she returned to the original topic, "it's your turn to dish about your detective. Because personally, I believe the guy would make an amazing addition to your mutineer/royal family gene pool."

"Not happening," Lani insisted. "And once again, he's not my detective."

But that didn't stop her mutinous mind, which seemed to have conspired with her reckless heart, to picture a Sunday morning walking on the beach, her holding hands with a bossy elder daughter in a flowered sundress and pink slippahs, who'd inherited Lani's own Irish- setter-red hair, while Donovan carried their dark-haired toddler son with eyes the color of a deep blue sea on his back.

The sun was shining, sea foam was kissing the soft coral sand beneath swaying palm trees, and it was just another perfect family morning in paradise.

And she was in so much trouble.

13

THE HONOLULU FBI office was located in an enormous four-story concrete and glass building with U.S., Hawai'ian, and FBI flags in front. Donovan paused at the interactive lobby display honoring agents who'd died in the line of duty. None, he noted, were from Hawai'i.

He was met by Mike Dempsey, the assistant special agent in charge, who, rather than the aloha shirt he'd been wearing when they'd met at the conference, was dressed in a dark blue suit, lighter blue shirt, and red tie. Which had Donovan grateful he'd gone with his gut and worn his own suit.

That Dempsey was proud of the building was obvious. He gave Donovan the grand tour, including the gun vault, which not only housed the weapons that SWAT and special agents would use but had a display of guns used by agents over the years, going back to the Thompson (Tommy) machine gun dating back to those days when special agents were known as G-Men.

The interrogation rooms were much like the ones Donovan, along with anyone who'd ever watched a television cop show, was used to, except for the handcuff bars that had been installed in the walls and a state-of-the-art computer with a touch screen that could immediately send fingerprints to be compared to those in the crime bureau archives.

"Okay. I have serious tech envy," Donovan admitted.

"Play your cards right and all this could be yours," Dempsey said. "We even have an MRAP in our vehicle annex," he added, referring to the military mine resistant ambush protection vehicle. "We used it on a multi-agency raid against a cockfighting and gambling ring."

After the tour, they got down to business over coffee, which, while not as good as what Lani had made him, was a lot better than the stuff he was used to at PPB. "So," Dempsey said, leaning back in his chair, "what can I do for you?"

Donovan gave him a condensed, but succinct version of the missing fiancé, the vandalism, and the supposed affair with an agent named Bob.

"We have two hundred agents here," Dempsey said. "Which is a far cry from when we opened a Hawai'i office in 1931 with one agent, only to close it three years later due to lack of crime. Which means, given the odds, we have at least one Bob. Probably more. But even if we do, and one of them happened to be on Orchid Island during that time period, you do realize I can't discuss an ongoing case with you. Unless you're operating in an official capacity."

"No, this is personal," Donovan said. "At the moment. But I get the sense that it's more than it seems. I don't suppose you can tell me if you've ever heard the names Taylor Young or Ford Britton."

Something passed across the agent's eyes. So quickly that had Donovan not been focused on them, he might have missed it. "I can neither confirm nor deny," he said.

"Let's try another way. If, speaking hypothetically, I find a reason for the FBI to become involved, are you guys available?"

"Our mission is to protect and defend the United States. Which would, naturally, include its citizens," Special Agent Michael Dempsey answered.

"That's what I needed to know," Donovan said, standing up and holding out his hand. "Thanks."

"Always happy to meet a fellow officer. Even if he is off-duty," the agent said. "And that was one helluva speech the other day. I learned a lot and hope you'll decide to join our ranks."

"I'm working on it."

"You're a shoo-in," Dempsey assured him. "If the powers-that-be weren't impressed, you wouldn't have been invited down here in the first place."

They shook hands again, the agent showed him out, and as he returned to the airport, Donovan put all thoughts of the agency and the missing fiancé out of his mind. As he focused instead on the night ahead with Lani, something that felt both good and dangerous at the same time moved in his heart.

14

LANI WAS ON her knees, applying mastic to the back of a piece of horizontal glass tile when she felt someone watching her. Already knowing who it would be, she made an attempt to stay calm but wasn't able to, and lifted her eyes. The hand she had lifted to rub the back of her weary neck dropped to her side.

"You're back," she managed, resisting the urge to leap on him, wrap her legs around his waist, and ride him into the paradise passion pit bedroom.

"I am. I like the tile." But his warm blue eyes weren't looking at it. They were looking at her, and his slow smile assured her that even though she was hot and sweaty, he liked what he saw.

"I'm glad."

"Where did you learn to do all this?"

Seriously? They were going to talk about construction? Now? When her eager ovaries were on the verge of exploding like Christmas luau fireworks? "Makaio Kuala taught me."

The tension in the air as he continued to look at her was beginning to make Lani's head throb. "He lives next door to my parents. I sort of grew up over there," she explained.

"The members of my family were always locked away in their various studios, being ultra-creative—Daddy with his horrible paintings, Mother with her sculptures, Nate with his stories—so, feeling like a fifth wheel a lot, I used to go visit Makaio."

She'd begun to babble. Because, dammit, he still wasn't saying a single word. Just standing there, eating her up with his deep blue eyes, which were turning to indigo.

"He's a local contractor; he built all our houses—my parents', this one, mine. I'm certainly not in his league, but he taught me everything I know. He's seventy-one years old. And still working."

"That's admirable," he said. "Seems island time leads to long lives."

"It does."

They fell silent again. Donovan leaned against the door-frame, his hands jammed into the pockets of his gray dress slacks.

"You know what I said about your suit?"

"You said a lot. None of it very positive."

"I take it back." She'd begun fiddling with the razor knife she'd been working with when he'd suddenly arrived. Which, now that she thought of it, was more than a little annoying since she would have liked to have had advance warning so she could've bathed, buffed, and polished for him. "You look pretty damn good, Detective."

"Not as good as you." His gaze swept over her in that slow, assessing way he had, not like a detective checking out a suspect but like a hot guy checking out a woman he wanted to bang.

And boy, was Lani beyond ready to be banged.

Her mind, which was already clouded with hormones, had been fantasizing about tying him to Nate's bed with that tie he'd loosened, when the blade slipped in her nerve-and-lust-dampened hand, leaving a gash across the tip of her index finger.

"Damn." She immediately stuck her finger in her mouth, which caused his eyes to flare. Then, his cop instincts set in as he was by her side in seconds, lifting her off her feet. But instead of carrying her into the bedroom, Rhett Butler style, and having his wicked way with her as she'd fantasized, he sat her down on the toilet and retrieved a Band-Aid from the medicine cabinet she'd recessed into the wall. Then he wrapped the wound, which thankfully hadn't taken off the tip of her finger because then he'd probably insist on taking her to the hospital, which was more of a clinic her father had established years ago.

When he appeared in no hurry to release her hand, Lani wondered if he could feel her trembling.

"Did you learn anything while you were on O'ahu?"

"Yeah. But nothing we need to talk about now. I'd rather talk about you. And all the things I decided while flying to Kaua'i, then taking the ferry to here that I want to do to you. *With* you."

"About time." She traced his lips with her fingertip. The SpongeBob SquarePants Band-Aid she'd bought as a joke for Nate took a bit away from the sexiness of the gesture, but when he cupped her face in his hands and kissed her, *really* kissed her (and wow, could Donovan kiss!), hot and hard and deep, with a lot of tongue tangling, as every part of her body began belting out "The Hallelujah Chorus," she forgot all about Bikini Bottom's most popular yellow resident.

The stiff scrape of Donovan's afternoon stubble was like the finest grade of sandpaper. No. She used a lot of sandpaper while working on this beach house, and none of it had felt as erotic as his face on his way down her neck, nipping at a spot right above her collarbone that Lani had never realized was an erogenous zone.

He lifted her, just as she'd fantasized, and this time carried her into the adjoining room and laid her on the bed. The fake fur was soft and lush against the backs of her legs.

"Damn."

His frown carved deep furrows in his brow. "What's the matter?"

"I hate it when my brother's right."

Donovan's answering chuckle came from deep in his throat, hitting her heart like an arrow. "You had me scared there for a minute," he said as he nuzzled her ear. "I thought you'd changed your mind."

"I have," she admitted, weakening as his fingers trailed lazily up the exposed length of her thigh. "Too many times to count."

"And?"

"And I keep coming back to the fact that I want you."

Donovan looked down into green eyes darkened with such open desire and felt the now- familiar movement in his chest. Over the years, he had come to think of himself as a rock—unemotional, immovable. Somehow, during their short time together, he'd discovered that he was a hell of a long way away from being the self-controlled, impervious man he had worked so hard to become.

Go with your instincts.

"That's convenient. Because I've wanted you from the beginning. You've been all I could think about from the first moment I saw you, with the sun striking sparks in your hair. I felt as if I'd been hit by lightning."

Lani stroked his cheek. "I felt the same way."

"And now?"

"As hot as you look, we need to get you out of those city clothes, Detective." After pulling the tie over his head, she grabbed a fistful of his shirt, ripped it open and raced her lips over his chest, causing him to groan deep in his throat before she was forced to stop when she hit the barrier of his damn belt.

Because his hands were steadier than hers, he unfastened it and yanked down his zipper, displaying a pair of crimson knit boxer briefs that confirmed what Lani had already figured out for herself. Donovan might be city detective cool on the outside, but he had a red-hot volcanic core.

Once they were finally skin to skin, she continued to plant wet kisses down the happy trail leading below his navel, but before she could create an eruption, he'd regained control and turned the tables, using his hands and mouth to burn heat everywhere on her body, until she was writhing beneath him, wishing she'd never taught him the concept of island time.

Then finally, just when she didn't think she could take any more, Donovan covered her with his beautiful body, and yes, she did grasp his very fine ass as he slid into her, fitting so perfectly, filling all those spaces inside her she hadn't even realized had been so empty, that tears came to her eyes.

And then, as he buried his face in her damp neck, and she wrapped her arms and legs even more tightly around him, there were no more thoughts.

•••

HAD IT BEEN hours or only minutes? Days or an eternity? Lani lay in Donovan's arms as she struggled to orient herself. The fiery glow of sunset had melted into yawning shadows that created deep blue silhouettes on the walls. Outside the open window, all was quiet as the birds settled down for the night. The only sounds were the rustle of palm fronds disturbed by the gentle trade winds and the soft sigh of the tide as it washed onto the beach.

"Okay," she purred, arching her back like a lithe, pampered cat, "I surrender."

Donovan ran a hand that had created such havoc to her body lazily down her side. "I thought you already had." There was no mistaking the satisfied smile in his voice.

"I was talking about the fact that any man who can make me feel the way you do could probably make me confess to anything. No wonder you're so good at your work, Detective."

He brushed a few strands of still-damp hair off her forehead and pressed his lips against her temple. "It's only been that way with you, Lani," he said truthfully.

Lani laughed as she turned in the circle of his arms and tangled her legs with his. "And isn't that exactly what you're supposed to say?"

"Seriously." His lips nibbled at hers as he punctuated his words with kisses that had her wanting him again. And again. "I've never met a woman who can make me lose control the way you do."

"I like the idea of being able to make you lose control," she decided as she trailed a slow, lazy finger up his inner thigh.

"If you needed any more proof..." Donovan took her hand and held it against the straining evidence of his renewed arousal. "You've been making me crazy from the beginning."

"You've got no idea how happy I am to hear that," she said, as she wrapped her fingers around him and drew him inside her. Where he belonged. "Let's be crazy together."

15

THE ENTIRE EASTERN arc of the horizon danced with fire as Donovan rose to greet the new day. A day, he had considered on first awakening, filled with possibilities. After the previous night, he felt himself imbued with almost mystical powers; whatever he wished for would be his. Whatever he sought, he'd find. Life was his oyster, Lani his pearl, and everything was coming up roses.

He laughed as he realized that he'd slipped from waxing philosophical into mixing metaphors. Both might be uncommon behavior for him, but this was a remarkably uncommon day. Even waking to an empty bed couldn't diminish his optimistic mood, because he had a good hunch where Lani was.

Wandering out onto the lanai, a cup of coffee in his hand, he saw her. She was strolling along the slender crescent of glistening sand, picking up the shells that littered the shoreline. The sea, illuminated by the rising sun, gleamed like molten metal almost too bright to look at.

Ah, but Lani was a different matter entirely, Donovan thought, his lips curving in an instinctive smile as he watched her pick up a shell, turn it over in her hand to study it intently, only to discard it. He could happily spend the rest of his life watching her do anything. Or nothing.

During the long and mostly sleepless night, she'd treated him to the massage her grandmother recommended.

While treated him to what turned out to be an incredibly sensual experience, Lani had explained that while technique was an important part of a Lomi Lomi massage, especially when used for healing as she was doing for his ankle, much of the practitioner's focus was on using loving hands and a loving heart.

Both of which Lani had in spades.

"People tend to think of memory and beliefs as stores in our head. In our brains," she'd said as her hands had moved over his body, spreading warmed coconut oil in long, continuously flowing strokes. "But Lomi Lomi belief contends that memory is stored in all the cells of our bodies, and that things like negative thoughts can block energy flow the same way as muscle tension can. And even if you don't buy into that belief, physically the massage relieves tension and stress and increases blood flow, which aids in the elimination of toxins."

Donovan had never been into woo-woo, although his partner had talked him into using psychics during the Cascades Killer hunt. None of whom had provided any helpful information. But he couldn't deny that his ankle felt better this morning.

As if sensing his gaze, Lani glanced up and smiled in a way that had him feeling he'd just swallowed the sun.

"Hi," she said a little breathlessly as she came up the wooden steps. "I couldn't sleep. But I didn't want to wake you."

"I wouldn't have minded."

Scattering her seashells on a nearby table, she framed his smiling face in her palms. "Ah, but I didn't want to wear you out."

He pulled her against him with one arm. "Do you think that's possible?"

"If last night was any indication, I'd say that was a no. In fact, if word of your stamina ever leaks out, you can say goodbye to your police career, Detective."

She glanced down at the cup he still held in his free hand. Steam rose invitingly into the tropical morning air, and the rich fragrance of the dark Kona coffee was enticing. "What are my chances of getting a cup of that?"

"After last night, you can have anything your warm little heart desires," he said, releasing her to return to the kitchen. "What do you mean, my career would be shot?" he asked as he made her a cup from the Keurig he'd opted for instead of digging out her French press.

"Thanks." She took a sip of coffee. "I was referring to all those scientists who'd track you down and lock you away in some laboratory while they sought to find the secret of your amazing virility."

Her eyes danced as she grinned at him over the rim of the mug. "If we could find a way to bottle whatever keeps you going, we'd make a fortune."

"No problem. The answer is simple." As his gaze turned suddenly dark, the way it had last night, when they'd been making love, Lani felt an answering warmth curling outward to her fingertips.

"It's you, Lani," he said with unnerving solemnity. "Only you."

Wouldn't it be lovely if it were that simple? Lani might have given up sex for Lent, but she was experienced enough to realize that something as rare as it was beautiful had passed between them last night. Something that if their circumstances were only different would have her shouting her love to the rooftops.

Simple? Hardly.

"Did you mean what you said? About not being in the market for a wife?"

Under normal circumstances, especially after last night, Donovan would have automatically taken Lani's surprising question as expecting some promise of commitment or permanency. But observing her strangely pale face, he had to wonder if she wanted assurance that their relationship was nothing more than a one-night stand. No, not that, he corrected thoughtfully. A vacation fling. A brief affair that would last only as long as his stay here on the island.

And why wasn't he relieved by that idea?

When he realized she was still waiting for an answer, Donovan did what any prudent man would do under the circumstances. He hedged.

"I didn't come down here looking for a wife, if that's what you mean."

"Great," she said with another of those dazzling sun-bright smiles. "I mean, that's good to know, because it occurred to me, as I was walking on the beach, that it'd be best to clear up any possible misunderstandings. That as amazing as last night was, I mean, I actually lost count of my orgasms, and believe me, that never happens, I'm certainly not expecting you to put a ring on it."

"Okay." Taking the mug from her hand, he put it next to the coffee pot, lifted her onto the counter, and proceeded to add to her orgasm count.

● ● ●

"Hungry?" he asked.

"Not as much as I was a few minutes ago," she said with a smile that only wobbled slightly. She'd always prided herself on not lying. Wasn't that why she'd had to leave Los Angeles? Truth, in her business especially, had been relative. But she'd definitely lied to Donovan when she'd led him to believe that she considered this time together merely a vacation fling. "But I could eat something."

Then minutes later, they were sitting out on the lanai, eating a breakfast of banana bread and fresh fruit.

"What did you find out at the FBI?" she asked.

"Nothing officially. But whatever your friend's fiancé is involved in, they know about it."

"You're kidding."

"Believe me, I never kid about the FBI."

"They told you that?"

"No. Because I was acting as a civilian on non-official business. But the agent I spoke with would neither confirm nor deny."

"And that told you they know?"

"It's cop speak. Like 'a person of interest.'"

She shook her head. "It has to be a mistake."

"It's not."

He sounded so sure of himself Lani had no other choice but to believe him. She also wondered if there was something he wasn't telling her, but suspected that if she pushed, he'd probably just give her that same line the FBI agent had given him.

She sipped her coffee, basking in the memory of being so thoroughly, expertly, loved. Donovan's lovemaking had been every bit as intense as the young man she remembered him to be before he had begun his successful series of career advancements. Which brought up something else she'd been thinking about on her morning walk.

"Why do you want to join the FBI?"

"Because they're the best."

His eyes were gleaming with the same light Lani had seen in Nate's eyes when her brother discussed his latest novel. Or when her father was in the planning stages of a painting. And her mother had taken on that same avid look while chiseling away on a piece of virgin stone. Able to recognize obsession when she saw it, Lani frowned as she spread orange marmalade on a thin slice of the warm, dark bread.

"What, exactly, do they do that you don't do now?"

"It's not that different," he admitted. "But at a national level. While I have to go through hoops to follow a trail outside Portland...Have I told you how beautiful you are this morning?"

"You have. Several times." She jerked her head back. "And you're dodging the issue. Damn it, Donovan, I'm trying to have a serious conversation with you."

He regarded her with that serious look he'd had when he'd first arrived. "I can see you are," he said calmly. "So, carry on."

"Thank you," Lani said. "Why did you want to become a policeman in the first place?"

It had been so long since anyone had asked him that question that Donovan had to stop and remember what had made him turn down an acceptance to medical school to enter the police academy.

He leaned forward, bracing his elbows on the chair arms as he considered her words.

"It's going to sound like bragging," he warned after a moment.

"Try me."

"I believed I could make a difference. That I could make the world, or at least my little corner of it, a better place for people to live."

"And, according to Nate, you've certainly succeeded." She sipped her coffee.

"If I haven't, it hasn't been for lack of trying."

Lani believed him. There was still one little point she didn't understand. "When was the last time you actually talked one-on-one with one of those people you wanted to help?" she asked quietly. "Unless it involved the crime you were working on?"

A puzzled frown darkened his brow. "I don't understand what you're getting at."

"I just was wondering if you've ever had time to mingle with the masses once you became a detective."

He studied her thoughtfully. "Why am I getting the feeling that you disapprove of my wanting to improve myself?"

Lani shrugged. "It's not for me to disapprove, Donovan. I have nothing to say about what you do with your life."

Donovan frowned. "That's what my ex-wife said. Right before she pointed out all the social disadvantages of my being nothing but a street cop."

Stunned by the intrusion of another woman into the conversation, Lani picked up her mug, staring into the dark brown depths as if the cooling liquid held inordinate interest for her.

"You were married?"

"For six months."

Lani had to ask. "How long have you been divorced?"

Donovan didn't want to talk about Kendall. Just thinking about his former wife gave him a sour taste in his mouth. "A long time. Her family and mine were friends and we married while I was still in pre-med. So, understandably, she assumed she was going to be a doctor's wife. She walked out the day I entered the police academy instead of medical school."

"So, you weren't married when we first met?" Donovan and Nate had spent so many off hours together, Lani thought surely a wife would have come up.

"We were separated and she'd already filed for divorce. I didn't blame her for feeling as if she'd had a bait-and-switch pulled on her."

"Her loss," Lani mused. "Why were you in pre-med in the first place?"

"Because that's what people in my family do."

"Excuse me? What does that mean?"

"You know how back when Catholics had lots of kids, every family seemed to give at least one to the Church as a priest or nun?"

"That was before my time," Lani said. "But we Breslins have had our share of priests and nuns in our family tree. But what does that have to do with you and medicine?"

"I didn't feel I had a choice."

"Donovan," Lani said, still uncomprehending, "of course you had a choice."

"Not really. Since I was an only child, it was up to me to carry on the Quinn tradition. My father's a neurosurgeon who invented some special brain stent that made him wealthier than he already was from family money. My mother's a psychiatrist, who, when I decided to attend the police academy instead of medical school, tried to put me on anti-depressants because she couldn't believe I was thinking clearly."

He'd also turned down the meds after Matt's suicide. While Donovan wasn't against better living through pharmaceuticals, he just hadn't believed either situation called for them.

He hadn't not gone to med school because he'd been depressed, but because he'd started meeting a lot of cops while volunteering his senior year at PSU in the ER. And although he'd admittedly been hit hard by burnout and his partner's death, just being here with Lani proved that he'd only needed a break. By the time the new year arrived, he'd be back to fighting shape.

Bored with talking about himself, which had never been one of his favorite things to do, he lifted her wrist to his lips and pressed a light kiss against her skin scented with the lotion she'd obviously put on this morning.

"You taste so good. I don't think I'm ever going to get enough of you. Come back to bed with me, Lani."

"As tempting as that is, I need to finish the tile in the bathroom. And, if I have time, patch your roof."

"Those things can wait. I seem to have been struck with the aloha spirit and want to spend the day with my wahine."

Lani couldn't think of anything she'd rather do. "What if it rains and your roof leaks?"

He shrugged uncaringly. "I've got that little problem all solved."

She lifted a russet brow. "Don't tell me that you're going to fix the roof?"

"Of course not. If there's one thing my work has taught me to be, it's a good administrator. And a good administrator always delegates."

"Delegates?"

"If it rains while we're making love, I'm delegating you to the top position."

"Gee, thanks," she drawled.

He pressed his hand against the back of her head, pulling her forward for an intense, explosive kiss. Stars glittered and spun on a backdrop of black velvet behind Lani's eyes, and she could have sworn she felt the distant rumbling of Mt. Waipanukai. But that was impossible, she told herself as her hands clutched Donovan's shoulders tightly. The volcano that had once served as Kealehai's home was now extinct.

"Wow," Lani murmured, tilting her head back to stare into his storm-filled blue eyes. "I think I feel an earthquake coming on."

"I feel it, too," Donovan agreed with a slow, inviting smile. "And as much as I'd love for us to make Richter scales go crazy all over the South Pacific, I need to go check out some stuff."

"Now?"

"You're the one who asked me to help find Britton," he reminded her. "I'd much rather stay here and rock the island with you."

"Later," she said on a long sigh. "I am worried about Ford. Even more so now that you believe the FBI's involved in whatever has happened to him."

"Later," he agreed reluctantly. "What's the name of the police chief on the island?"

"Manny Kanualu."

"I think I'll pay Chief Kanualu a little visit." Donovan rubbed his jaw. "Professional courtesy, and all that. And afterward, I'll check out The Blue Parrot, since that's where Ford supposedly hung out."

"Taylor's telling the truth about that," Lani said. "Call me when you've left the police station, and I'll meet you there."

"Sorry, sweetheart, but this is something I need to do alone. Not that you're not an intelligent woman, but I've spent more time questioning people than you have. You wouldn't want to tip any bad guys off, would you?"

"Of course not. But what am I supposed to do while you play cops and robbers?"

"You can always finish up my tile," he suggested.

Lani's answer was a brief, pungent curse.

16

"WELL? WHERE'S YOUR young man?" Margaret's bright eyes observed Lani with interest.

"He's on his way to the police station. Then some sleazy waterfront bar for thrills and adventure," she muttered grumpily. "And he's most definitely not my young man."

The elderly woman chuckled. "Try telling that to him," she advised. "And while you're at it, would you care to explain why even the mention of Donovan Quinn makes you blush?"

"This isn't a blush," Lani insisted. "I never blush."

"Of course you don't," Margaret agreed knowingly.

"It's this room; it's like a rain forest in here."

The purple head bobbed. "It is nice, isn't it?" Margaret's pleased gaze circled the room, enjoying the colorful display of tropical plants.

Recognizing her chance, Lani changed the subject to her grandmother's ingenious green thumb. For the next five minutes they discussed the spectacular crimson blooms of the royal poinciana, the lacy pink and white shower trees, and a new night-blooming cereus Margaret had acquired and had high hopes for.

Unfortunately, Lani was soon to discover that her reprieve was only temporary. With the tenacity of a bull terrier worrying a particularly succulent bone, Margaret deftly returned the conversation to its initial topic.

"You and Donovan are lovers, aren't you?"

Knowing her grandmother's penchant for speaking her mind, Lani tried not to take offense at the forthright question.

"Really, Tutu," she protested with a weak smile, "that's a very personal question."

Margaret tilted the Belleek shamrock teapot, filling their cups. "It doesn't matter. If you haven't made love yet, which, I'd bet my Golden Globe that you already have, there was enough electricity between the two of you to set this entire island on fire."

"There's no future for me with Donovan Quinn."

Still-bright eyes, sparkling with intelligence, looked straight into Lani's. "Are you telling me that you're not going to take him as a lover because he hasn't promised you fifty years of married bliss?"

She made it sound so easy, Lani mused. And why not? She had no doubt that if her grandmother had found herself in Lani's position, she would have reached out for whatever Donovan had to offer with both hands. Margaret Breslin lived for the moment. In that respect, Lani had believed that the two of them had shared a lot in common as she, herself, had breezed through the past few years taking one sun-filled day at a time.

It was coming as a distinct surprise to discover that she was not quite as carefree and impulsive as she had thought. Somehow, when no one was looking, the no-nonsense, practical stock of Thomas Breslin's New England whaling ancestors had slipped into the family's gene pool, ultimately ending up in her.

"I'm not like you, Tutu. Yes, you undoubtedly had love affairs over the years. But you had one grand passion in your life, which resulted in my father. And when that relationship was over and Palmer Winfield dutifully returned to his wife, the automobile heiress, you threw yourself into your work and never looked back. No recriminations, no regrets."

The sudden rattling of the delicate china cup against the saucer captured her attention, and Lani was appalled to realize that her hands were trembling.

Margaret sat up on the peacock throne chair, her elderly spine as erect as if someone had slipped a rod of cold steel down the back of her lace dress.

"I take back what I said about you being bright," she shot back, her eyes blazing. "You're a fool if you don't think I had regrets. Recriminations? My God, I loved Palmer—I adored the ground that man walked on. I thought I was going to wither up and die when he left me."

For just a fleeting moment, as Lani observed her grandmother with surprise, she was able to see the young woman who'd obviously experienced many of the same unsettling feelings that Lani herself was currently suffering.

"But you didn't."

"No. As you already pointed out, I had my work. And of course, I had your father."

She reached out and covered Lani's hand with her own beringed one. Blue veins crisscrossed the back of Margaret's hand, but her still-soft skin was the color of gardenias, free of the age spots so many of her contemporaries suffered. As Lani lifted her gaze to her grandmother's face, she thought how the former Hollywood sex goddess was still a remarkably beautiful woman.

"Don't let the mistakes of the past stop you from loving, darling," she said with a sudden, almost desperate urgency. "I'm old enough to have known a great many men. Donovan is one of the good ones. I know it in my heart. And unlike Palmer, he isn't married."

"Donovan *is* different," Lani agreed quietly. "He's like no one I've ever known, and when I'm with him, I feel like a different person...No," she said, "that's not it. I do still feel like myself. Just better. More fulfilled."

Comprehension dawned in Margaret's eyes. "You're in love with him."

"No. I don't know. It's so fast...But maybe I am," Lani admitted.

Avoiding her grandmother's sharp gaze, Lani shifted her attention outside the glass walls, toward a scarlet cardinal that was perched on a twisted branch of a pandanus tree, seeking shelter from the slanting silver drops.

"Would that be so bad, Lani?" Margaret asked gently. "What's the worst that can happen?"

"You really want to know?" Lani's eyes were burning with tears she refused to shed. "What if Donovan falls in love with me?"

"I can think of worse fates."

"What if he wants to get married?"

"I'll dance at your wedding," Margaret said without missing a beat.

She didn't understand, Lani thought miserably. "Can you see me living in Portland? Or following my husband around from posting to posting? Doing whatever it is FBI agents' wives do? I've lived off island. While it was fun for a time, looking back, I realized that like seemingly everyone else there, I was playing a role that wasn't a good fit for me. Like if you'd been cast in the Faye Dunaway role in *Bonnie and Clyde*."

"If I'd been younger, I would have rocked that screenplay."

"I've not a single doubt." But it would have been an entirely different movie. And that was Lani's point.

"I enjoyed many parts of my work," she allowed. "I liked researching and writing questions. It was like changing to a new major every day. I liked taking care of the *Beauty* contestants. But at the end of the day, I was never truly happy. Nowhere near the way I am here. I don't want to ever do that again. Not even for Donovan."

Margaret didn't argue. "Then he'll simply have to move here, dear," she said calmly.

Would that it was that easy. Lani was well aware that all of them, herself included, lived in a fantasy land of their own making. Her grandmother, along with her mother, brother, and yes, even her father, had created this special world by their artistic efforts. Citizenship in the magic realm had been Lani's birthright.

But Donovan was only a visitor here. When his vacation was over, he'd be returning to the harsh world of reality. Alone.

"Well," she said as she got up to leave, "we'll never know what Donovan would do, will we? Because I'd couldn't ask him to give up something he's worked his entire life to achieve. So it's a moot point."

She bent down and kissed her grandmother's weathered cheek. "Thanks for the tea, Tutu. It was delicious, as usual."

Margaret beamed. "Wasn't it? If you weren't already destined to be with your detective, I'd spend whatever time I have left fixing you up with Kai. He's going to do wonders with our tea farm and will need a special woman with your imagination to be a partner in the project."

"It's going to be wonderful."

As she drove back to Nate's beach house, Lani also considered how it was that a woman in her nineties could remain so focused on her future, while Lani, herself, was wearing blinders, limiting herself only to the present.

But if that's all she could have...

She was debating her and Donovan's situation when the rain suddenly stopped as if turned off at a tap, and a rainbow appeared over the rising green ramparts, painting the sky with bold strokes of colors.

As the vivid, sun-kissed arc banished clouds of despair, Lani vowed to grasp this positive feeling and hold on to it. Because whatever her future held, sunshine or showers, she was going to enjoy the moment.

17

DONOVAN WAS AWARE of Lani the instant she entered the waterfront dive. Every head in the place swiveled in her direction as she stood in the doorway, allowing her eyes to become accustomed to the dim light. When she finally located Donovan, she smiled and crossed the room to the bar and climbed up on the empty stool next to him.

"What the hell are you doing here?" he asked beneath his breath.

"Having a drink with you," she murmured back. "I'll have a mai tai," she said, raising her voice to give her order, and a dazzling smile, to the bartender.

"I don't remember giving you permission to come here."

"No surprise, since I don't recall asking for permission," she said easily, thanking the bartender with yet another of those siren smiles as the man with colorful ink sleeves and a prison teardrop tattoo beneath his left eye placed the drink in front of her.

"That glass probably hasn't been washed in a month," Donovan warned as she took a sip of the cool rum drink.

"That's all right," she answered as she was obviously fighting back choking on the fruit and rum drink. "There's enough alcohol in here to kill any bacteria that might be fool-hardy enough to stick around."

"Speaking of foolhardy—"

Lani placed a placating hand on his arm. "Don't be mad. I really did try to stay away. I even went up to my grandmoth-er's house. But I couldn't stop thinking of you here. Alone. Possibly in danger."

He shook his head as he lifted the longneck beer bottle to his lips. He'd learned long ago that when forced to drink in places like The Blue Parrot, it was safest to stick to beer. "So you decided to make things dangerous for both of us. Makes sense to me."

"I'm a woman of many interests," she reminded him. "Along with my eclectic college education, I also happen to have a second-degree brown belt in judo."

"Good for you." It was admittedly impressive. It also showed a dedication to study that didn't surprise him. But there were also cases when a little knowledge could be a dan-gerous thing. And this could well end up one of them. "So when was the last time you used your judo skills in a real life-and-death situation?"

"Taylor's right," she muttered, which answered his ques-tion. "You *are* mean. All I wanted to do was to be with you. Do you have any idea how bad I'd feel if you suddenly disap-peared like Ford?"

"I'm not going to take off and leave you without saying good-bye, if that's what you're worried about."

"But you *are* leaving." Damn. Lani could have bitten off her tongue as the incautious words escaped her lips. It was the rum. She'd always thought places like this watered their drinks. Then again, when you were pouring the equivalent of kerosene, you probably had a better profit margin.

Apparently sensing her discomfort, Donovan softened his tone. "You knew all along I have to go back to Portland."

"For goodness' sake, Donovan, there you go again, taking things too seriously." Her desperate green eyes circled the room, not pausing to light anywhere.

"This is so much fun," she gushed with feigned gaiety. "I feel just like Castle and Beckett. With you being Beckett, of course. If she were male. Which, of course, she wouldn't be, because then it would be an entirely different program." Cue the babbling. What did this man do to her brain?

Donovan was watching her carefully. "Lani—"

Lani refused to acknowledge the concern in his steady gaze, knowing that to do so would prove her downfall. "Have you found out anything about Ford?"

"Not a damned thing," he muttered. "It appears the aloha spirit hasn't quite reached The Blue Parrot. At least not when it comes to a mainlander."

"Haole," she murmured. "Perhaps I can help."

Before Donovan could stop her, Lani slid off the stool and made her way to the end of the bar, where a group of dockworkers were standing in front of a flat-screen, playing a video game that appeared to involve a great deal of gratuitous violence.

"Hey, brah," she said in a silky, sultry voice that made Donovan, as he came up behind her, want to drag her right out of the bar. Now. "Any of you know where I can find da kine scuba man, Ford Britton? Haole here wanna take diving lessons." She jerked her tawny head in Donovan's direction.

"Wasetime to look for him here," an affable giant with arms the size of tree trunks answered in the relaxed pidgin English Donovan had been hearing since entering the bar. "Mo' betta you find his ipo, Wainani...girlfriend," he elaborated for Donovan's benefit.

"Taylor Young's scuba man's ipo," Lani corrected.

"Scuba man been makin' fastime with a new ipo," the man insisted. "Dat lady got mo' dolla than can count. Scuba man buy drinks for the house udda day. He say by'm'by he be a fucking rich man."

Lani couldn't believe Ford would leave Taylor for another woman. Even a rich one. "*Mahalo*," she murmured absently as she considered this new aspect of Ford's disappearance.

As the man's dark eyes skimmed down Lani's body with unmistakable interest, Donovan slipped a folded bill into the pocket of the dock worker's flowered shirt. "Thanks," he said.

After checking out the denomination of the bill, the man's face lit up in a broad grin that was missing a front tooth. "Hey, brah, *mahalo* yourself."

When he noticed two guys at a nearby table watching them closely, Donovan grasped Lani's bare upper arm. "Come on, sweetheart. It's time to go."

"But I haven't finished my drink."

"Yes, you have."

"Really, Donovan," she complained as she found herself being unceremoniously hauled out of the waterfront bar. "Has anyone ever told you that you can be very bossy?"

"All the time. And I do my best to live up to it. Now if you don't mind, I'd like to get out of here before those Feds come to the mistaken conclusion that we know more about all this than we do."

"Feds?" Lani looked back toward The Blue Parrot as Donovan practically dragged her across the parking lot. "As in FBI?"

"Not the IRS," he agreed grimly. "Although at this point, I wouldn't be surprised to find out that they had a hand in all this, too."

"Had a hand in what?" Lani asked, clearly confused.

"Give me the keys to the Jeep. We'll come back for the rental car later."

"Okay," she murmured distractedly as she dug the key ring out of her purse. "What's going on?"

"I don't know," he said as he shoved her ungently into the Jeep. "But I'm sure as hell going to find out."

They drove for a while in silence, immersed in thought.

"By the way," Donovan asked, "where the hell did you get that dress?"

Lani smoothed the skirt of the red sarong-style strapless dress that could have been sprayed on. "I borrowed it from a friend who dances in a show at one of the resorts on Maui. I didn't have anything that looked appropriate for a place like The Blue Parrot," she added as an afterthought.

"That's a relief."

"What's the matter? Don't you like it?"

"You look freaking amazing. Even if you did look as if you were trolling for Johns," he tacked on. "The guy sitting next to me practically fell off his stool when you strolled in the door."

Lani's face lit up with a bright smile. "Why, Donovan Quinn, I do believe that you're jealous."

"I just don't like you looking like the sort of woman who belongs in that kind of place," he muttered.

She leaned over, running her fingers through his hair. "Hey, brah," she murmured silkily into his ear, "you wanna come over to my place, find out da kine woman you got?"

Donovan caved, as she'd known he would. He ran his hand up the long expanse of leg bared by the deep slit in her skirt. "Lady," he growled seductively, "thassa mo' betta offer than I get all day."

18

"IT'S A BOAT," Donovan said suddenly as he and Lani lay together, arms and legs tangled, in her bed after having, what she'd assured him, was primo, number-one sex.

He'd also discovered that the Hawai'ian pidgin could sound really sexy coming from those luscious lips, especially when she used dirty words that didn't need any translation.

It was the first time they'd been together in her place and the minute he'd walked into the beach house, he'd decided it definitely suited her. The bleached wood floor reflected the light of the Orchid Island sun, bathing everything in a warm yellow glow. The furniture was light and airy white wicker and rattan, the cushion covers printed with a brilliant tropical print.

Flowers were everywhere—scarlet and gold hibiscus blossoms floated in a pair of bright blue ceramic bowls, and branches of purple bougainvillea and snowy-white oleander were stuck haphazardly into colored, one-of-a-kind bottles. On the sunshine-yellow walls, a veritable garden of oversize tropical flower prints bloomed within the borders of narrow aluminum frames.

The entire atmosphere in the small house—the furniture, the flowers, the whimsical goddess figurine made from the leaves of the hala tree—was as free-spirited and unpretentious as its owner. As different as it was from his modernistic Portland apartment, Donovan was surprised to find himself feeling at home.

"What's a boat?" Lani asked, snuggling up against him, her head on his chest.

"*Wainani.* She's not Britton's new girlfriend. She's a damned boat."

She looked up at him. "How on earth did you come to that conclusion?"

"It only makes sense," he argued. "Look, he's a scuba diver, right?"

She nodded. "Right."

"And he knows these waters pretty damned well."

"Like the back of his hand."

"Let's say, just for argument's sake, that while he's out diving one day, he runs across a sunken wreck."

"One with treasure on it," Lani said, warming to the idea.

"Exactly. So he concocts a plan to get the loot off the boat without anyone knowing."

"But Taylor finds out and turns him in to the FBI?" she asked skeptically. "I'll admit she appears to be lying about what she knows about all this, but a woman can tell when another woman's in love. And Taylor is definitely in love with Ford. She'd never do anything that would risk getting him arrested. No matter what he'd done."

Lani shook her head firmly. "I'm sorry, but that piece just doesn't fit at all, Donovan."

"Sure it does." As his eyes gleamed with enthusiasm, Lani decided that she loved watching Donovan's detective mind work. "Let's assume that Britton told Taylor about the ship," he continued patiently. "Or that she got suspicious enough about all his absences to break things off."

"She told me she'd considered calling off the wedding," Lani allowed.

"Which underscores my point. So, taking the matter one step further, let's also suppose that the cargo, whatever it is, belongs to the U.S. government."

"All right. So far I'm with you, but..."

Lani's voice trailed off as comprehension suddenly dawned. This must be like how Nate felt when he was plotting a book. "Next chapter...

"Since Taylor loves Ford, she doesn't want him to go to prison. So, without telling him what she's doing, she goes to O'ahu to talk to the FBI, and without giving any details, tries to find out if they'd be willing to pay a reward."

"A finder's fee," Donovan agreed. "That way—"

"Ford gets more money than he'd make in several lifetimes with that diving business of his, he stays out of jail, he and Taylor get married, and both of them live happily ever after," Lani said.

"That's a workable scenario. It would also explain why she never contacted the local police yesterday," Donovan agreed. "She's obviously trying to protect him and figured the Feds pull more weight."

That last was certainly unwelcome news to Lani. "Taylor didn't contact the police?"

"Nope. Chief Kanualu didn't know anything about the vandalism."

"Yet another piece of the puzzle pointing to Taylor knowing what's going on," Lani admitted reluctantly. "But I still don't believe she knows what's happened to Ford. Otherwise, why would she involve you? And go to the FBI?"

"Good question." He reluctantly pushed aside the top sheet that was barely covering her tan body. "Come on, sweetheart, we're wasting time. Let's go check the harbor records."

"For sunken ships?"

He ruffled her hair with an easy familiarity. "You are not only one drop-dead sexy wahine, you plenny primo detective, Lani Breslin."

• • •

"WHERE DID I ever get the idea that police work was exciting?" Lani complained on their second day of searching through the stacks of leather-bound journals, seeking some record of the *Wainani*. Unfortunately, Orchid Island hadn't yet digitized all their records, which dated back to the 1700s

"Despite what you've seen on television, most of it is painstaking detail work," Donovan said. "Like looking for the proverbial needle in the haystack."

"Well, we couldn't have found a dustier haystack if we'd tried," she complained, wiping at a smudge on her pink T-shirt. "Whatever happened to the computer age?"

"You're the one who pointed out that things are a little slower here," he reminded her as he skimmed through yet another thick journal.

"I know." Lani sighed. "But it seems so hopeless, Donovan. What if it turns out that the *Wainani* isn't a boat, after all? We will have wasted two valuable days of your vacation."

"It's a boat," he reassured her confidently. "And as for my vacation, I'd never consider any time spent with you wasted."

She managed a weak smile. "Sometimes you can say the nicest things. Thank you. I needed that right now."

She sounded tired and uncharacteristically discouraged. Reminding himself that Lani was not used to spending her days in dingy basement storage rooms, searching for the single key that might unlock an entire case, Donovan put the heavy book aside and went over to her.

"Did anyone ever tell you that you look terrific with dirt on your cheeks?" he asked as he ran his knuckles over her cheekbone.

"You're just prejudiced."

"Probably so," he agreed easily. "But you still look gorgeous in dirt."

"If you find this appealing, you should see me covered in mud."

A flame sparked in Donovan's dark blue eyes. "Now that's an interesting idea. Have you ever considered taking up mud wrestling?"

She arched a brow. "With you?"

He bent his head to kiss her. "Of course. You don't think I'd let you go rolling around in the mud with anyone else, do you?"

"Mud's awfully messy," she murmured as his lips brushed enticingly over hers.

"I know. That's precisely why it's supposed to be fun. And why guys like it."

When she tilted her head back to look up at him, the familiar dancing light was back in her eyes. "And exactly who's going to clean up all the muck afterward?"

Donovan laughed. "There you go again, revealing that surprising practical streak," he complained good-naturedly. "Want to go home and take a long shower for two?"

She twined her hands around his neck. "Funny you should bring that up. I was just thinking the same thing."

Feeling the now-familiar stir of desire, Donovan kissed her long and lingeringly. "Later," he said reluctantly.

"Later," she agreed with a lack of enthusiasm that mirrored his own.

They had been back at work for less than ten minutes when Lani found it.

"Donovan!" she called out excitedly. "Here it is! The *Wainani*! She went down in a tropical storm nearly fifty years ago on a trip from O'ahu to Orchid Island. You were right."

"So she was a cargo barge," he read over her shoulder. "Let's see what's on the manifest."

"Just the usual," she murmured, reading through the lengthy list. "Tools, hardware, cars—" As she turned the page, Lani drew in a sharp breath. "And the sugar cooperative's monthly payroll in the vault!"

"The cooperative shipped two hundred and fifty thousand dollars in cash?"

"It wasn't all that unusual," she explained. "The workers, many of whom were transitory, didn't really trust banks. Most of them preferred to get their pay in cash. And continued to until after 9/11, when the island tax department got stricter and started cracking down on untraceable payments."

"No wonder Britton was jazzed," Donovan mused. "A quarter of a million tax-free dollars, while not exactly the kind of loot that was on the Titanic, would still make a nice nest egg for anyone to start a marriage with." He frowned as he continued to read the record. "This is interesting."

"What?"

"The Coast Guard received a distress signal right before the *Wainani* went down."

"What's so unusual about that?" Lani questioned. "They probably receive a lot of SOS calls during storms."

"Probably do," he agreed. "But how many of those ships do you think report that they're being boarded by pirates?"

"Seriously?" Every vestige of fatigue vanished as Lani's eyes filled with excitement. "Pirates?"

"Pirates. But don't get that excited because I seriously doubt we're talking Captain Jack Sparrow…It's time we had another little talk with Taylor."

"This is getting more thrilling by the minute," Lani said as they returned up the coast. "Imagine the *Wainani* being boarded by pirates only minutes before it went down with all that cash on board!"

"Now all we have to do is find out who hired the pirates."

She glanced over at him. "And you can do that, can't you, Donovan?"

He grinned as he patted her thigh. "Piece of cake."

Her face was flushed, her eyes bright, reminding him of the way she looked when they were making love. Although Donovan had been dragged into this case, he wasn't feeling so bad himself.

After being cooped up behind a desk for so many years, coming in after crimes had been committed, he'd forgotten the thrill of the chase. Only two things dampened his enthusiasm: the first being that he still didn't have a clue as to Britton's whereabouts and the second was the nondescript sedan that had been following them all day. A quick glance in the rearview mirror confirmed that it was still there.

"What's the matter?" she asked.

"It seems Dempsey knew a lot more than he admitted to me," he said. "Because we've been followed all day."

"By the FBI?"

"Hopefully. And don't turn around," he said when she began to shift in the seat. "I'd rather it be the Feds than whoever's after Britton."

• • •

"Pirates?" Taylor stared at Donovan as if he'd suddenly started speaking Martian. "The *Wainani* went down with pirates on board?"

"The fact that you know the name of the ship suggests you also know what your fiancé's been up to," Donovan said.

"Only some of it," Taylor insisted. "I knew he'd found the ship and intended to salvage it. But I didn't know anything about pirates. And I certainly don't know where he is! Pirates?"

The last was said with a wail, and her hands shook as she attempted to light a cigarette. She'd finally managed to quit last year, but Lani decided it wasn't surprising that this situation would have kick-started the habit again.

"Here," Donovan said, taking the matches from her hand. "Let me."

Taylor gave him an appreciative look as she inhaled deeply. "I was afraid you'd find out about the *Wainani*," she said on a flat voice. "Especially after Lani told me all about you being recruited for the FBI."

"I thought you wanted Donovan to find Ford," Lani objected.

"I did. Because I was getting desperate. He was my only hope. I just didn't want him to find out about the *Wainani* at the same time."

Lani was clearly confused. "Why? Surely you don't think Donovan would steal the money?"

"Of course not." Taylor was on her feet, pacing nervously back and forth across the floor of the candy shop that looked a lot tidier than it had just two days ago. She'd locked the door and turned over the Closed sign as soon as they'd arrived. "But I was afraid if he knew what Ford intended to do, he'd arrest him."

"My jurisdiction doesn't cover Orchid Island," Donovan pointed out.

"So?" She shot him the stink eye. "All you'd have to do is tell Chief Kanualu what you know, and Ford could end up in jail."

"Donovan wouldn't do that," Lani said quickly. "Would you, Donovan?"

"I'm a lot more interested in keeping the guy alive than in putting him behind bars," he confirmed. "Speaking of which, what, exactly, did you tell the Feds?"

"I didn't think you'd bought that story about the hookup," Taylor admitted. "I knew it wasn't very convincing, but I had to make up the story on the spot. How was I to know that you'd find out I'd been to Agent Dempsey's office?"

"I told you he was brilliant," Lani put in.

"So you did," Taylor agreed dryly. "As for the FBI, I didn't give them any details. I only asked Dempsey and the two other agents he called in, if the government gave rewards for the recovery of stolen salvage. Hypothetically, of course."

"And you thought they'd buy that?" Donovan asked. As many years as he'd been a cop, he'd heard just about everything. And could still be surprised at the idiocy of some people.

Taylor nodded. "They certainly seemed to. In fact, they didn't appear at all interested in anything I had to say."

Donovan knew better, but he didn't see any point in muddying the waters at this point. Since Taylor had actually been cooperating for once, he didn't want to take a chance on her clamming up.

"Where is the *Wainani*, Taylor?" he asked quietly.

"I don't know. Ford said it would be safer if he was the only one who knew where she went down," she added, seeing Donovan's disbelieving look.

"Do you know if he had a chart showing the spot?"

Taylor shook her head dejectedly. "I don't think so. That's what the people who trashed our shops were looking for, wasn't it? The chart."

"It would appear so," Donovan agreed.

"I was so worried about the authorities finding out what Ford was doing. But the men who tore the place apart weren't FBI, were they?"

Donovan's lips were a taut, grim line. "No. They would've shown up with a warrant."

Her blond hair was like a curtain, hiding her face as she bent her head. When she finally lifted her gaze, her wet eyes observed Donovan bleakly. "Ford's in a great deal of danger, isn't he, Donovan?"

Donovan knew the gallant thing to do would be to lie, to assure Lani's friend that she'd have her missing fiancé back in time for dinner. "I think he is, Taylor," he said instead.

She digested that for a long, thoughtful moment. "Then you'll just have to find him before something terrible happens to him."

"Of course he will," Lani assured her. "Won't you, Donovan?"

"Since I've always been a sucker for gorgeous damsels in distress," Donovan said philosophically, "I suppose I don't have any choice."

"Taylor is beautiful, isn't she, Donovan?" Lani asked as they drove away from the Sugar Shack.

Knowing he was in a no-win situation, Donovan merely shrugged. "Sure. I suppose so. If a guy goes for that type."

She slanted him a sideways glance. "Don't most men prefer blondes?"

"Not necessarily. And I thought we'd agreed that I'm not most men. Are you by any chance fishing for compliments?"

The blush that was the bane of every redhead's life rose brilliantly in her cheeks. Folding her arms, Lani directed her gaze steadfastly out the window. "Of course not. Don't be silly."

He reached over and took her hand. "For the record, the gorgeous damsel in distress I was referring to was you."

A smile lit her eyes. "Thank you, Donovan. That's a very nice thing to say."

"It's the truth," he said simply as he glanced up at the rearview mirror, not at all surprised to see the sedan still following at a discreet distance.

19

THE CAR CONTINUED to stick with them later that evening, parking nearby when they attended a showing of Thomas Breslin's paintings at the Orchid Island Gallery. Donovan had been to several gallery shows over the years but none as unique as this one.

The white walls were covered with abstract paintings, all of which were as colorful as they were horrendous. Watching Thomas circulate through the crowd, drinking in the enthusiastic compliments, Donovan decided that he had never seen a happier man. To no one's surprise, it appeared that the show would sell out before a family dinner at the Breslin home.

"Would you be very angry at me if I showed up a little late to the dinner?" Donovan asked, taking Lani aside. She'd glammed up for the occasion in a dress-style version of a Chinese tunic, slit on the side to reveal an enticing glimpse of golden thigh. The blaze of color would have put a bird of paradise to shame. "I need to slip away for a short while."

"Of course not. I can always get a ride with Mom and Dad. Or Margaret and Kai, who'll be joining us, since he's essentially become part of the family. Where are you going?"

"I want to try to get a line on those pirates."

"Tonight? Won't the trail be awfully cold?" Lani privately prided herself on knowing the proper investigative jargon. All those years of faithfully watching *Magnum P.I.* and *Hawaii 5-0* every week were beginning to pay off.

"I suspect Britton's probably heated it up," Donovan replied.

"Donovan, people know you're looking for Ford. You could be in danger, too."

"Don't worry. I know what I'm doing."

"And what, exactly, are you doing?"

"Going back to The Blue Parrot," he informed her reluctantly. It was bad enough that Lani had walked into that dive in the middle of the afternoon. He damned well didn't want her showing up there at night.

Despite his reassuring words, Lani was overcome with a growing sense of anxiety. "Not alone, you're not."

"I'm not taking you with me, Lani. Not this time."

"But—"

"No."

Lani had spent enough time with Donovan to know when arguing would be fruitless. He was, after all, a professional. And the FBI didn't hire pushovers. She put her hand on his arm. "Promise me you'll be careful."

Donovan decided it was nice to have someone worry about him. "Absolutely." He kissed her. "See you in a bit."

Lani seemed about to say something else but instead merely nodded. Despite his reassuring words as he left the gallery, she couldn't forget that night so many years ago when he had crept through a dark and dangerous warehouse. Alone.

• • •

THE CLIENTELE DIDN'T seem to have changed, but the shifts must have, because there was a different guy behind The Blue Parrot's bar. The anchor and eagle tattoo on his forearm went along with the aloha shirt printed with various U.S. Navy ships.

"I was wondering when you'd get back," he said, when Donovan sat down on a stool. "Adam, he'd be the bartender you met earlier, told me you and Lani had been in here looking for my cousin."

"You're Ford Britton's cousin?"

"Yeah. He was born on Kaua'i, but he's spent a lot of time since high school skipping around the islands. My name's Nick."

He proceeded to explain a complex line of family connections that Donovan didn't even try to follow, but being a hot shot soon-to-be-special-agent detective, he'd already figured out family ties meant a lot more on this island than they did in other places.

"And you'd be Donovan Quinn. Nate's detective friend from Oregon."

"News gets around."

"When you're on an island, it goes round and round and round," he said. "I'm guessing you haven't met my cuz?"

"No. He'd already gone missing when I arrived on the island."

"Yeah. I heard Taylor hired you. Which kind of pissed me off, because she could've come to me, being that I'm also a law enforcement professional, but I guess she was afraid I'd feel obliged to tell the chief."

"You're a cop?"

"Yeah. It was a natural fit being that Uncle Sam decided to put me into Shore Patrol. Which comes in handy working here from time to time. If there's anything that gig teaches, it's how to handle drunks…You going to order anything?"

"I wouldn't turn down one of those bikini beers."

"The Bikini Blonde Lager," Nick said. "Not a bad choice. It's a bit of a sleeper craft beer from Maui. One could argue it's more like a Kölsch than a German Helles lager, but it's a nice, easy American brew." He popped the cap and set the yellow can with a hula girl on it in front of Donovan.

"Though, having been in the Navy myself," Nick continued, "I seriously question their slogan about it being what sailors really come to shore for. Personally, I came for the women."

"Yet you obviously know your beer."

"Beer came in a close second," he admitted with a grin that revealed a lot of memories. "I'm a home brewer now. Working to get into it full time once I retire, which hopefully is sooner, rather than later, which is why I'm moonlighting three nights a week here. And speaking of beers, from what you've learned about Ford, you've probably figured out he's a few bottles short of a six-pack."

"He appears to have made some mistakes."

"There's family talk that his dad tripped over the dog and dropped him on his head bringing him into the house from the hospital. I'm more in the camp that believes he's just never grown up because he's the baby of the family, a mama's boy, and no one ever made him take responsibility for anything. Personally, I think Taylor would be better off dumping his fool ass, but no way am I going to play Dear Abby in that relationship.

"I did, by the way, tell him he was being an idiot not going through the proper channels when he found that ship."

"You know about it?"

"Sure. This place was packed for ladies' free Jell-O shot night when he got hammered, blew out his limit on his Visa buying a round for the house, talking about how that ship was going to be rich."

"I was told he was talking about a new, rich girlfriend."

"Yeah. But the guy who told you that isn't a whole lot better in the gray-matter department than my cousin. He'd also been tossing back a lot of tequila shots that night, so I wouldn't give a lot of veracity to anything he might say.

"About a week after that, these guys came looking for him. They were obviously not local cops, or I'd know them. And they sure as hell weren't FBI. After they drove off, I ran their plates, then got their ID info from Kenny, who'd rented them the Buick. I put their names in the federal database back at the office, and they popped up connected to some mob guy in Honolulu. Who, in turn, has ties to an extended family of wise guys in Arizona."

"What families?"

"The Tsukasa family on the island. Capelli in Phoenix."

Donovan recognized the names immediately. The Tsukasa were a branch of the Japanese transnational Yakuza syndicate, and he'd been after the Capellis this past year when it was discovered they'd moved into Portland as a way station between the States and western Canada.

"Shit."

"That's putting it mildly. If Ford isn't careful, he's going to end up shark bait for sure."

"Sounds like you think he's still alive."

"They haven't turned the car back in yet. So, yeah, I'm guessing they're still looking for him." He gave Donovan a look. "I haven't been able to find him, and believe me, I've been talking to all the usual suspects, so I'm guessing he's been taken off island. Which gets complicated for me, because I'm still a cop, meaning that I'd have to check in with any other jurisdictions, and you never know who's working for whom."

Which, as much as Donovan hated to admit it, was true. Sometimes people you expected to be the good guys had gone over to the other side, where the pay was a helluva lot better.

"But if you're going to save his sorry dumb ass," Nick said, "it'd better be fucking soon. Because we're talking a ticking clock here, brah…Want another brew?"

"No, thanks." Donovan threw some bills on the bar. "I've got a dinner to get to."

"At the Breslin place." He put the cost of the beer into the box masquerading as a till and shoved the rest of the money in his pocket. "Lani's a nice woman. We were sort of a couple for a few months our junior year in high school. I played wide receiver on the Mutineers. She was voted head cheerleader."

Of course she was, Donovan thought. Not because she was beautiful, which she was, and not because her family was royalty, which was weird to think about, but they were, but because she would have been just as friendly and cheerful as she was now. If he'd been getting pounded on a football field every Friday night, he sure as hell would've felt a lot better looking over and seeing her waving her pom poms on the sidelines.

•••

ALTHOUGH HE KNEW Tess would probably yell at him for being a chauvinist cop, on the drive up the coast from The Blue Parrot, Donovan decided not to tell Lani what Nick had shared about the mobster who'd hired the pirates. The pirates had gone down with the ship, but Donovan knew they would've been expendable. It was the cash the guys were looking for. Not because a quarter of a million dollars was what it once was. But from what he'd been able to tell, when he'd worked organized crime, the bad guys had long memories and held grudges all the way to their graves.

When the time came to confront the hired goons, which he hoped would be sooner rather than later, Donovan didn't want Lani anywhere in the vicinity.

She threw herself into Donovan's arms when he arrived at the house. "Do you have any idea how worried I've been about you?"

"I told you I could handle things," Donovan reminded her.

"I know. But I was still going crazy." She ran her hands over him, as if searching for hidden injuries. "Are you sure you're all right?"

"Positive. Although if you want, we can go somewhere more private, and you can check me over for broken bones."

Her eyes were bright with both relief and desire. "Remind me of that offer when we get home."

"You've got a deal."

"Did you learn anything that will put us closer to Ford?"

"Nothing."

"Oh, dear. And we were getting so close."

"Don't worry, something'll turn up. It always does. Here—I brought you something." He bent to pick up the gift bag he'd dropped when she'd jumped him.

"Oh, Donovan," Lani murmured, as he slipped the lei over her head. "What a lovely surprise."

"The woman at the shop told me that the ancient chiefs used these flowers to make leis for Kealehai, so I figured they'd be perfect for you."

Her fingers plucked the feathery scarlet ohia lehua blossoms. "They used to be considered sacred," she said softly. "Thank you."

He shrugged. "I like buying you things, Lani."

His words were simple, but the sudden solemnity of his tone threatened to be her undoing. Afraid she'd break into tears, she took him by the hand and led him into the solarium, where the family had decided to wait for his arrival. Greetings were exchanged, a drink was pushed into his hand, and although Margaret was nothing but gracious, Donovan got the feeling that she knew a secret she wasn't sharing.

"Speaking of buying things," Lani murmured, after they'd sat down for dinner. "Everyone appreciates what you did this evening at the gallery."

"Buy three of your father's paintings?" Donovan asked with a shrug. "That wasn't being nice; I liked them."

She glanced down at the glass of rum in his hand. "How many of those things did you have at The Blue Parrot before coming here? Those paintings were the worst of the bunch."

"They couldn't have been," he said, playing with her thigh through the slit in the skirt beneath the tablecloth. "They were all of you."

"How on earth could you tell?"

"Simple. I looked at them, felt the heat, and knew it couldn't be anyone else." He tilted his head. "Have I told you that you look absolutely *nani* this evening?"

Lani had noticed that, little by little over the days, native words had begun to slip into Donovan's vocabulary. That grim business-suited man she had first seen struggling along the beach had undergone an amazing metamorphosis into the Donovan Quinn who was now sitting beside her. Donovan was wearing a white polo shirt—she still hadn't managed to talk him into a flowered aloha shirt—depicting a trio of surfers across his broad chest while showing off firm biceps and a pair of loose white pants. The expensive Italian loafers had given way to a pair of practical beach sandals. All in all, Lani thought that Donovan had never looked better.

He was gradually succumbing to the philosophy of *hoomanawanui*—let's take it easy—with an ease that almost had Lani believing he could be happy here in paradise. With her.

"*Mahalo*," she answered. "You don't look so bad yourself," she said. "For a *malihini*."

His fingers skimmed higher, creating sparks on her leg. "Ah, but you're prejudiced."

Lani caught his hand before things got dangerously out of control. "You bet I am."

• • •

As THE FAMILY enjoyed after-dinner conversation out by the pool, Thomas drew Donovan aside, inviting him into the solarium.

"I think I owe you an apology," Thomas surprised Donovan by saying as soon as they were alone.

"An apology?"

Before he could answer, Lani's father's phone pinged. He pulled the phone from his pocket and read the text.

"I'm afraid I'm going to have to leave," he said. "Debbie Akana's baby was due last week. She's on her way to the hospital now."

"It must keep you busy, maintaining a general practice."

"It's an around-the-clock job," Thomas agreed cheerfully. "But I love it."

"Do you ever regret not specializing?" Donovan asked, genuinely curious. Although family practice had made a comeback of sorts in the past few years, general practitioners were still a minority.

"I did specialize," Lani's father corrected Donovan amiably.

"On Orchid Island?"

"New York," Thomas corrected. "I was chief of surgery at Mount Sinai."

Okay. That was one of the biggest surprises anyone in the colorful Breslin family had thrown him. "How could you leave a prestigious position like that to deliver babies on some remote island?"

Thomas's smiling face sobered. "At the time, I wasn't sure that I could," he admitted.

"But then one day, Kalena asked me if I was happy."

His expression softened, and Donovan had the feeling that Thomas Breslin was back in the hustle and bustle of New York City. "Damnedest question she'd ever asked," he murmured, as if to himself.

"Were you?"

"To tell you the truth, I'd never stopped to consider whether I really liked what I was doing. From the time I entered college, I just kept sticking to the plan I'd made for myself. Medical school, internship, residency..."

"It took Kalena to point out that I was turning into an automaton. Turn the key in the morning and I'd go to the hospital, where, each day, I became more of a mechanic than a doctor. I never really knew my patients. I only knew their hearts or their gall bladders or their kidneys.

"So, figuring I had nothing to lose, we packed up Kalena's chisels and my black bag and moved back here to my childhood home, where I began seeing patients as people again. Now I know enough to make sure that there's a night-light in the room when little Keoke Santos has his tonsils out because he's been afraid of the dark since he got lost in that lava cave last year.

"I also know that I'd better pick up some lemon drops for Debbie before I go to the hospital because her husband, who usually supplies her with them, has been stuck on the Big Island all week at National Guard camp.

"Regret not specializing?" he repeated. "I am specializing, Donovan. In people." He flashed another quick, warm, eye-brightening grin that reminded Donovan of his daughter's. Then he headed out to buy lemon drops and deliver a baby.

Leaving Donovan to ponder Thomas Breslin's unexpected family story.

20

THEY DIDN'T MAKE it to the bedroom. They were no sooner inside her cottage than Donovan pulled Lani into his arms and pushed her back against the door, holding her there by pressing that hard, magnificent body against hers. Then, with hands as deft as a surgeon's, he yanked up her dress and ripped away the thong panties she'd bought solely for the intention of driving him insane by strutting around the bedroom wearing just the scarlet-as-sin dental floss and a barely there scrap of lace demi bra.

She mourned the ridiculously pricey ripped panties as they flew onto the table where she kept her keys, only for a mere nano-second, because, at the same time, his wickedly clever mouth was kissing her senseless. If there were an Olympic medal for kissing, Lani thought, as her own hands dragged down his pants, Donovan Quinn would take the gold.

Her dress up around her waist, his pants bunched around his ankles, he lifted her off her feet, right out of the high-heeled backless red sandals.

"Put your legs around me," he instructed, his breath sounding as if he'd run a marathon, which was more than she could say for herself, because Lani wasn't sure that he hadn't kissed every last bit of breath right out of her lungs. "And hang on."

His palms cupping her bare butt, and her back still against the door, he thrust into her, crushing his body against hers while she wrapped her legs around his waist, grabbed hold of his hair, and went along for the ride of her life, which, when it ended nearly as soon as it had begun, left her seeing stars.

"I think we're in trouble," she managed to gasp as every muscle and bone in her body went limp, causing his knees to buckle from her dead weight as he struggled not to drop her onto the bamboo floor.

"Unhook your legs," he groaned against her throat. Which she did, sliding down his body as if he were a firepole. "Okay." He staggered, managing to catch her beneath the arms before she hit the floor. "We've got this."

"Thank God," she said, as they both slowly, gingerly folded to the sisal rug, which, even as scratchy as it was, felt better on her butt than the damn thong had. "I would have died of embarrassment to have Johnny Mahuiki see me naked again."

"Who's Johnny Mahuiki? And do I have a reason to be worried?"

"He's the island's EMT, and if an ambulance has to be sent out, the odds are he'll be on it. He's also my cousin and we used to take baths together when we were babies. I was too young to remember it, but our mothers took pictures."

"Pictures? You have naked pictures of yourself?" he asked, making her laugh.

"My mother does. And if you dare ask to see one, you'll never have sex with me again." She rolled over on top of him. Partly to get off the rug and partly because she wanted to feel his body against hers. At least the good parts that weren't still covered by clothes.

"I hope Dad didn't bore you tonight," she said.

"He sure knows a lot of art history." Donovan wrapped his arms around her.

"Which he's always happy to share and may have been useful if I were still writing questions for *Jeopardy!*."

"I quit paying attention when he got to the Etruscans," he admitted. "Because I was having a debate with myself."

"About what?" Starting to feel frisky again, she began nibbling his neck, pleased to discover that she wasn't the only one ready for round two.

"About whether or not I should make you come over dessert."

"You could not!"

"Oh, I knew I *could*." He ran a hand over her butt and squeezed. "The question was whether or not I *should*."

"So, what stopped you from trying?" As wicked as the idea was, Lani couldn't deny it was tempting. If they'd been anywhere but with her family...

"I wasn't sure you could keep from moaning and screaming my name the way you always do when you come."

She lifted her head and looked down into his laughing bad-boy eyes that were such a change from the sad, shadowed ones he'd viewed the world through when he'd first arrived.

"I do not."

"Yeah, you do, and believe me it's hot as hell. In fact, if you're ever looking for yet another job, you could probably make big bucks as one of those 1-900 phone sex women."

"Do they still have those? With all the Internet porn available?"

"They do. I guess because not everyone has a computer handy, and some guys actually like to use their imaginations. When I was working vice, I had to listen to way more than any human ear or brain should have to handle. But believe me, sweetheart, you top them all."

"I can't decide whether to be insulted or flattered."

"I meant it as flattery. Your mother's right about you having your own talents. But that one's probably inappropriate for a family dinner."

"I still don't believe you."

"Want to move this party into the bedroom and I'll prove it to you?"

"That's assuming either one of us can move."

"Oh, ye of little faith. Roll over again, and, being the strong, manly alpha male cop that I am, I'll help you up."

Which he did. Then, holding on to each other like two drunks leaving The Blue Parrot at closing time, they managed to make it to the bed, where Donovan proved his claim. Apparently, all the previous times they'd made love, she'd gone not only blind, but deaf, because she'd certainly never heard herself making those wild woman noises before.

"You do realize," she said, as she snuggled up to him, her head on his chest, her long legs wrapped around his muscular, hair-roughened ones, "that you've handed me a secret weapon."

"Oh?" he asked, his absent tone revealing that he hadn't made it all the way back to reality yet as his hands, which had learned her body well, idly stroked their way from her shoulders, down her back, and lower. "What's that?"

"I'll demonstrate my new super powers. Ready?"

"Go for it," he said.

"Oh, Donovan," she gasped in a breathless, throaty tone. "Please, Donovan...Please...Do that again, baby...Oooh! Yes! Yes! Yeesss!" After an ear-piercing scream, she let out a long, slow, moan that softened to a silky, satisfied purr.

"Okay," he said. They both looked down at the already renewed hard-on that had him thinking she could possibly kill him if they kept this up. Not that he was complaining. Because right now he couldn't think of a better way to go. "That is one helluva a super power. But I just happen to have a few of my own."

Before she could question what powers Donovan possessed that could possibly equal the one she'd just proven, he planted a row of wet kisses down her body, spreading her thighs apart with his wickedly clever hands so his mouth could fully claim sensitive, still-tingling parts. Then, with a stroke of his tongue, finished her off. As she shattered, Lani did, indeed, shout out his name.

"I think," she decided, when she could talk again, "that when it comes to super powers, it's a draw."

"Works for me." He drew her close into a spooning position, put his hand over her breast, and as she heard the steady breathing that told her he'd fallen asleep, she let her own eyes drift shut.

The last thought Lani had, as she fell into sleep, was although she must have written dozens of topic answers about famous lovers, for the first time in her life, she actually knew what true love felt like.

21

WHILE WAITING FOR the feelers he'd put out on Britton—
who'd seemed to have vanished from the face of the
earth and hopefully wasn't swimming with the sharks as the
bartender had suggested—the day after his visit to The Blue
Parrot, Donovan discovered that Lani wasn't exaggerating
about the Island's Christmas celebration.

While the mainland Americans might be dreaming of a
white Christmas, Orchid Island had its own unique take on
the holiday. The parade was much the same as ones happening in most places in the world. The floats, many covered in
flowers, were lit with white and colored lights while girls
waving flags and pom poms marched along with the high
school band. Also marching were uniformed Girl and Boy
Scouts while military vets going back to World War II either
marched or rode on floats that garnered the most cheers. The
route wound through the town, past sidewalks filled with
families, most dressed in holiday-themed attire, ending at
the beach in front of the Breslins' home.

Which was where Kanakaloka, aka Santa Claus, dressed
in a red-and-white poinsettia aloha shirt, red board shorts,
and a traditional red Santa hat arrived in an outrigger canoe

with dolphins swimming alongside, to hand out brightly wrapped gifts.

The trunks of all the palm trees had been strung with bright lights, and a play snow zone had been set up at the end of the beach with, Thomas informed Donovan, twelve tons of the icy white stuff he'd had shipped in.

"What's the point of having money if you don't use it to make others happy?" he asked Donovan, proving yet again the difference between Lani's family and his. His own parents were spending Christmas in London this year. Last year was Paris, and the year before that, they'd gone on a Greek Island cruise.

A late, unplanned child, Donovan had never been mistreated. His childhood had been more of benign neglect, beginning with a series of nannies, housekeepers, and boarding schools.

Watching the snowball fights taking place, he decided that these laughing, shouting, shrieking kids would rather be here, with family and friends, than getting a golden ticket to Disneyworld.

"Your dad certainly pulled out all the stops," Donovan said as he watched, at the very edge of the battle zone, another smaller, quieter group of children industriously building a snowman that would doubtfully last the night, but tonight, there were no cares nor thoughts about tomorrow. There was only now. Island time.

"In ancient times, the islands celebrated *Makahkiki*, a New Year festival that covered four lunar months from the fall into February or March," she explained. "It was to honor the god Lono, and the bounty of the land. During those months, all wars were forbidden."

"A season of peace and goodwill to all men," he said.

"True. But that was a concept impossible to explain to the Protestant missionaries who arrived in the 1820s with their own ideas of proper religious practices," she said. "Since they banned ancient gods, most of what we celebrate today came from them." Although her voice had sounded a little sad about the loss of an ancient tradition, she smiled. "Of course, the missionaries, mostly from New England in the early days, didn't have a king who could bring in snow, so they undoubtedly missed their white Christmases."

Local merchants had donated items for a raffle with funds going to the local food bank. Taylor had contributed a huge basket filled with an assortment of her bestselling candy, while Thomas had provided a signed oil painting depicting a trio of dancing dolphins wearing Santa hats. It had been painted, Lani told Donovan, during her father's Oceana stage.

So many people had lined up to buy tickets you'd think they were giving away free *musubis*. Lani had bought him one of the sandwiches consisting of a fried slice of Spam on rice pressed together into a small block, then wrapped in seaweed, from a street vendor. She'd assured him that not only were they the most popular to-go snack in the islands, eating one was a rite of passage for any malihini (newcomer) aspiring to achieve local status.

When the sun sank into the Pacific in a blaze of color, the night became alive with fire and music while long tables draped in red and green linens were covered with platters of food. If Donovan had found Orchid Island to be a different world than the mainland, tonight he felt as if he'd stumbled into a DeLorean and gone two hundred years back in time.

Flaming torches glowed a brilliant orange against the star-studded black sky as the throbbing beat of drums echoed the pounding of waves against the dark lava ramparts. The sultry night air was perfumed by myriad flowers adorning the huge backyard, their hues rivaled by the brilliant aloha shirts, dresses, and brightly flowered muumuus, which, Lani told him, were updated adaptions of the voluminous Mother Hubbards, which those early missionaries had forced on the indigenous population.

Greetings of *Mele Kalikimaka* were exchanged, many directed to him, as, Lani suggested with one of those sunny laughs he'd come to love, people were checking him out to make sure he was good enough for her.

Then, suddenly, the deep, foghorn sound of the conch shells being blown encouraged increasingly loud answering roars from the gathered crowd.

"They've just taken the pig from the imu," Lani said, pointing toward the subterranean oven, where Donovan could practically feel his arteries clogging from the aroma alone. "The first recorded Hawai'ian Christmas was in 1786, when the merchant ship, the Queen Charlotte, docked on Kaua'i. The captain and his crew celebrated with a big dinner, including a whole roasted pig, which started a new tradition that spread through the islands."

She linked her fingers with Donovan's, leading him from the shadows into the circle of light created by the flaming torches where he found himself seated between at the head table between Lani and Thomas, facing an extraordinary array of exotic dishes.

"I like this," Donovan said after taking a taste of the opihi, a salty black mollusk that reminded him of a small clam.

"Try this lomi lomi salmon," Lani suggested, holding out a piece of the pink-fleshed fish.

"You've just caught my interest, sweetheart," he said, thinking of her massages. Not only were they helping his bum ankle, since the first one, he hadn't suffered any more nightmares of his partner's brains and blood looking like a Jackson Pollack painting splattered on the wall.

"In this case, the salmon's massaged with a marinade of chopped onions and tomatoes before cooking."

Donovan's lips closed around her fingers. "Good," he decided. "But I think I prefer Lomi Lomi Lani."

Her eyes darkened with memories of the lovemaking that had inevitably followed the massages. "You haven't tried the poi," she murmured.

"I'll try it later," he said, toying with the natural pearl adorning her earlobe.

"You haven't experienced a real luau without tasting poi," she insisted.

Without taking his eyes from hers, Donovan dipped two fingers into the wooden bowl of purplish-brown starch made from pounded taro root. It tasted like library paste.

"Terrific," he said. "Can we go home now?"

Thomas, who had been arguing with Margaret over whether the chicken luau was better with taro or spinach leaves, overheard Donovan's request.

"Oh, you can't leave yet," he insisted. "The dancing's just beginning."

Donovan sighed as he ran his knuckles down the side of Lani's face, trailing his fingers along her firm, uplifted jaw. "Later."

"Later," she agreed, sensuality swirling in those sea-green eyes.

"The hula began as a religious dance," Lani remarked, reverting to her best tour-guide fashion. "It reflected the deep cosmic piety of the people, their love and awe of the tremendous forces of nature that surrounded them."

The percussive rhythms that accompanied the dancers came from wooden sticks struck together, producing sounds like those of a xylophone. Other musicians clicked together small stones like castanets, or shook seed-filled gourds to the pulsating beat, reminding Donovan of Latin-American maracas.

"You're supposed to watch their hands," Lani explained. "They tell the story."

A lissome young thing whose undulating hips were tracing a perfect figure eight momentarily captured Donovan's attention. "You watch the hula your way and I'll watch it mine," he suggested with a wicked grin.

Lani laughed. "It's just a good thing I'm not a jealous woman, Donovan Quinn, or you'd end up with this bowl over your head and poi dripping off your chin."

Before he could assure her that she had no reason to be jealous, that she was the only woman he wanted, she was called away for her dance.

"The story Lani will be telling will be a more modern one than the other legends," Thomas told Donovan as Kalena left with Lani to help her change. "Of the mutineers arriving on the beach and being welcomed by the local population. It's a grand tale and Lani interprets it in her own special fashion."

• • •

"I KNOW YOU'RE going to tell me it's too soon. But I'm so in love with Donovan, Mama," Lani admitted to her mother as she changed into her costume in her old room in the house.

"Hearts have their own time, just as islands do," Kalena said. "And I'm so very happy for you. What did Donovan say when you told him?"

"Oh, I haven't yet. He's been so occupied with Ford's disappearance, I didn't feel the time was right."

"From what I've noticed, while I'm sure he's working hard on the case, he's far more occupied with you."

"It's just physical." Lani cringed. "Which, I'm sorry, is TMI when talking to my mother."

"If I wasn't familiar with lovemaking, we wouldn't be having this conversation," Kalena responded mildly. "Can I take from the fact that you haven't said anything to him, that he hasn't told you that he loves you?"

"No, but he told me that he's never felt the same way with any other woman. And I can feel it." She splayed her hand over her heart. "Deep in here. If he doesn't quite know he loves me yet, I'm willing to be patient. Because he will. Because we belong together. Just like you and Daddy."

Concern filled Kalena's eyes, but she smiled as she wrapped her arms around her only daughter, her baby, who'd changed during her time away but had re-learned to laugh, and yes, even risk her heart again since she'd returned home.

"I've always loved your enthusiasm for life, darling," she said, as she fastened the pearl button at the back of the silk halter top that was admittedly a bit more revealing than the usual traditional costume. "And it's obvious that you've had quite the positive effect on Donovan. But sometimes people aren't exactly on the same page."

"If he isn't, he'll get there," Lani insisted. "I'm willing to wait until he does." And then, because it was Christmas, and she wasn't going to allow negative thoughts to intrude, she tied the matching silk sarong skirt low on her hip, then drew in a long, deep breath, then let it out, finding her center, as Ona Chang was always reminding her to do in meditation class.

"You'll see, Mama. It'll all turn out wonderfully, and one of these days, before you know it, you're going to be a grandmother."

Just the thought of making babies with Donovan had Lani smiling as she ran out of the house and onto the stage to the introduction of the drums.

22

SHE'D CHANGED FROM one of her flowered sundresses into a silky top that bared her shoulders and arms and a sarong thing that fell to mid-calf. Having already been informed that traditional hulas had been for religious purposes, and therefore the wahines dressed more conservatively than women did in the tourist luau dances, Donovan immediately decided that 1) Lani didn't need a grass skirt to be sexy and 2) he had never realized it was possible for hips to move in the way she was moving hers.

As the story played out, a young, hot man, his oiled body, clad only in some sort of wrapped loincloth, jumped in front of her, representing, Thomas informed him, the arrival of the mutineers.

Her hips moving erotically in a way that had him thinking of Sam Goldwyn's quote about her grandmother's filling theaters, Lani danced up to the guy. Then, taking off the red poinsettia Christmas lei she was wearing, she placed it around his thickly muscled dark neck. As the music increased its pace, her hips matched the rhythm, as did the male dancer, who was a great deal more physical, leaping around, stamping his bare feet in what was obviously a mating dance. Which, while making Donovan hot, also had him experiencing something that felt uncomfortably like jealousy.

When she danced off the stage, the male following, Donovan didn't need a program to know that what came next in the real-life version, would be the sexual union that had created the island's population.

Then she was back, standing in front of him, holding out her hands and giving him the most dazzling, bone-melting smile he'd ever seen.

"Dance with me, Donovan?"

Glancing around, he realized that while he'd been engrossed in watching her, others, around him, including her parents, had risen to their feet and were doing their own interpretations of the hula. None of which could hold a candle to hers.

"How could I refuse anything you'd ask?" He stood up. "And for the record, you were definitely off the mark when you said you didn't have any talents. I can't remember when I've seen anything as sexy as you doing that hula."

"I'm glad you liked it," she said, wrapping her arms around his neck and leaning against him, swaying to the music in a way that had the quickening beat of the drums pounding in Donovan's veins.

"What would you say to continuing this party at home?" he asked hopefully.

She went up on her bare toes to kiss his mouth. "Detective, I thought you'd never ask."

•••

THE CALL CAME shortly after two a.m. Lani dragged her hands through her sex-and-sleep-tangled hair as she listened to

Donovan's end of the conversation from the other room. His short, cryptic statements told her nothing.

"Who was that?" she asked after he'd hung up.

"Nobody important." He pulled on some jeans. "Go back to sleep."

"If it wasn't anyone important, why are you getting dressed? And what are you doing with that?" Her eyes widened as he pulled a pistol out of the dresser drawer and stuck it in the back of his belt.

"I've got to go out for a while."

"Where?"

"Just out. I'll be back before you know it."

The gun was the deciding factor for Lani. "I'm coming with you," she said, throwing back the sheet.

"The hell you are."

"Donovan, you only got involved in this entire mess because I talked you into helping my best friend. Think how I'd feel if you were hurt."

"Think how I'd feel if *you* were hurt," he responded gruffly. The very idea sent ice water into his veins. He grabbed her arms. "Don't you understand? I care about you, Lani. So damned much."

His intense expression made her stomach flutter. It wasn't the L word. But he was coming closer. "I care about you, too, Donovan. And I promise not to get in your way. But please let me come with you."

As he looked down into her earnest face, Donovan felt as if he were drowning. "Dammit, this is crazy."

"If you don't let me come, you know I'll follow you to wherever you're going."

He scrubbed his hand wearily over his face. What had ever made him think he could keep this woman from doing whatever she wanted to do? Donovan was well acquainted with Breslin stubbornness, since her brother possessed more than his share. While Donovan had always admired Nate's tenacity, he was finding Lani's frustrating.

He also, for the first time, understood how Nate had felt when Tess's life had been in danger.

"When we get to the island, you're staying on the plane," he said in his toughest, I'm-the- big-bad-detective-and-you'll-damn-well-do-what-I-say voice.

Sensing his acquiescence, Lani began to throw on her clothes. "What island?" she asked as she pulled a black T-shirt, the better to go unnoticed in the dark, over her head.

"The one where they're holding Britton. Do we have a deal or don't we?"

"Whatever you say, Donovan," she returned sweetly. "Ford's been here in the islands this entire time?"

"Apparently. When he sobered up and realized he'd mouthed off in the bar, he did a vanishing act and hop-skipped from island to island hoping to put everyone off his trail. It took the goons working for the syndicate who had hired the original hit on the *Wainani* this long to track him down. From what I could find out, they're holding him until their boss arrives here tonight from the mainland."

"If they're holding him captive, then they don't know where the *Wainani* is," Lani said thoughtfully.

"Probably not. It's obvious that they ransacked the shop looking for the sea chart. Britton must have done something right for a change and hidden it in a place none of us have thought of."

"It appears so. What island is he on?"

"Tern," he answered, naming one of the northwestern leeward islands.

"Tern Island? But that's a wildlife refuge."

"Then these guys should feel right at home," he countered. "Are you ready?"

"Almost. Won't it be difficult to hire a plane and pilot at this hour?" she asked.

"We won't have to, because I've had one waiting at an old deserted airfield for the past eight hours."

"What a lucky coincidence," she murmured, "that you'd hire a plane this very evening. Even after your visit to The Blue Parrot supposedly didn't turn up anything very valuable."

"I found out Britton was probably being held on one of the uninhabited islands," Donovan admitted. "But I didn't know until that phone call exactly which one."

"You lied to me, didn't you, Donovan?" she asked calmly.

"It was more a lie of omission. One I thought was best."

"Don't you think that was rather presumptuous of you?"

The movement of his jaw suggested that Donovan was grinding his teeth. "If it's presumptuous to want to keep you alive, then yeah, I guess I was being presumptuous." He glanced pointedly at his watch. "We're wasting time here, Lani."

She gave him an acquiescent smile as she pulled up a pair of black pants. Okay, so, being yoga pants, they weren't all that practical, but they were the only dark ones she owned. "I'm ready whenever you are, Donovan."

His only response was a muffled oath, but as they walked out to the Jeep, Lani thought she detected a ghost of a smile on his tight lips.

When they reached the airfield that was little more than a patch of dirt, Donovan led her directly to a Piper Apache parked at the end of the runway. When the pilot—a grim-faced man in his mid-to-late thirties with a military haircut—saw Lani, he scowled.

"Don't tell me that you're bringing a woman." His disapproving tone showed exactly how little he thought of the idea.

"She'll be okay," Donovan assured him. "She'll be staying on the plane."

"It's your funeral," the pilot muttered with a shrug as he turned his attention to preflight details.

"Nice crew you've hired," Lani said to Donovan as they boarded the twin-engine plane. "If the pilot's any example of the hospitality on this airline, I can't wait to meet the flight attendants."

"It's a no-frills flight," Donovan said, ignoring the snark. "We're going to have to serve ourselves."

Lani paused as she buckled her seat belt. "Don't mind if I do," she murmured, leaning over to give him a kiss. "Whatever can I do to thank you for including me in this adventure?"

"I'll accept that as a down payment," he said, brushing his thumb against her lips. "We'll discuss how you can pay off the rest of the debt once we get back home."

Lani wondered briefly if Donovan had noticed his slip of the tongue in calling the beach house home. Deciding that this was no time to bring up what was a perilously personal question, she nodded.

"Whatever you think is fair," she agreed, as the pilot climbed into the cockpit of the small four-seater plane. Within minutes, they were airborne.

"You know, of course, that your girlfriend's marrying an idiot," Donovan said as they raced through the night. Outside the windows, the sky was filled with brilliant, twinkling stars, and down below, the silver moon-gilded water seemed to go on forever.

"I'll admit Ford never seemed overly brilliant," Lani agreed. "But don't you think you're being a bit hard on him?"

"Not nearly as hard as that syndicate boss is going to be if we don't get to him first."

"You said he was coming from the mainland?"

"From Arizona," Donovan said. "Joe Capelli's a ruthless Mafia don who grew up in the Phoenix Scorsese and Marino crime families and has been moving north into Nevada, Idaho, and the Pacific Northwest and Canada. We've been trying to get something concrete on him for months while I worked on a money-laundering case with Tess.

"We put away one of the low-level guys, but we couldn't get any further than that, which frustrated the hell out of Tess, who was prosecuting both cases. I sure as hell never expected to nail the guy down here." He shook his head. "Funny thing is, the family had apparently written the barge off as a loss years ago."

"Until Ford got drunk and told everyone in The Blue Parrot that the *Wainani* was going to make him wealthy," Lani guessed.

"Got it on the first try," he said.

"But why would a mobster care that much about the money? Granted, it's a lot to most people, but surely it's not even a day's income for him."

"Those guys don't like losing. They're also greedy as hell. I've seen unlucky gamblers beaten to death for a lot less. It's no accident that Phoenix was considered the most violent city in the country when the Italian, Irish, Chinese, Japanese, Mexican, and Russian gangs were battling over territory there in the early 2000s."

"I'd honestly hate your job," she said. "But it's no wonder the FBI wants you."

He wrapped his arms around her. Right then he didn't want to think about going to the Feds. He didn't want to think about Britton, the crime boss, or the damn pirated payroll. He only wanted to remember how perfectly Lani Breslin fit in his arms.

"Look at those stars," he murmured. "You never see stars like that in the city. Too many lights."

"And smog," she whispered as she rested her head on his shoulder and tried to relax. "How much longer?"

"Not long. There's an old navy landing field dating from World War II on the island; these days it's used to deliver supplies to a small group of Coast Guardsmen stationed on the island to broadcast signals to ships and planes to help them plot their positions.

"As soon as we land, I'll go in and get Britton. The whole thing should be over in ten, fifteen minutes. Then you can start thinking about ways to pay off your debt."

"Donovan," she began hesitantly, "about my staying on the plane—"

"No." He gripped her chin, holding her gaze to his. "No arguments, Lani. We made a deal, and I have every intention of holding you to it."

She reached up, rubbing at the deep lines that bracketed his mouth. "Has anyone ever told you that you're very sexy when you're doing your alpha male thing?"

"Dammit, Lani—"

"Perhaps if we discuss this reasonably, we can find a middle ground."

"After this is over, we can discuss it all you want. For the rest of the night, I'm the boss."

Lani recognized the tone instantly. Further arguing was going to get her nowhere. "Of course, Donovan," she answered mildly. Almost, as hard as it was, submissively. "Whatever you say."

He was looking at her suspiciously when the pilot called out that they'd reached their destination. As they landed, Lani's heart felt as if it might leap right out of her chest.

Donovan didn't trust Lani's atypical acquiescence, but short of tying her up, he didn't know what to do except give her one last warning. "Remember, whatever happens, you are not to leave this plane," he ordered gruffly.

She dipped her bright head. "I'll wait right here."

Donovan wished he could believe her softly issued promise. Back at the beach house, he'd reluctantly believed her intention to follow him to the airfield. Where, he'd known, she'd try to convince him to take her along. Even if he'd managed to resist that appeal, she probably would have just gotten a boat to take her to Tern Island. At least this way he knew where she was.

Wearing a pair of night vision goggles he'd bought on O'ahu, he located the shack at the northernmost end of the island. It was precisely where his informant had told him it would be. From what he could tell from his vantage point in the bushes, there were no guards posted outside. So far, so good.

Making a motion with his arm, he instructed the pilot, who had accompanied him, to go around the back of the house and wait for his prearranged signal. Without a word, the man drifted into the shadows.

Donovan glanced down at the illuminated dial of his watch. There was still time before he would make his move. He was just congratulating himself when he heard a bush rustle. A moment later, Lani slipped up beside him.

"Dammit," he hissed furiously. "What the hell ever happened to keeping a promise?"

"I had my fingers crossed. Is Ford in there?"

"Yes. Now get back to the damned plane."

"I'm not leaving you," she whispered firmly. "I'm sorry, Donovan, but I've given this a great deal of thought and came to the conclusion that I couldn't bear not knowing what was happening to you."

Another quick glance at his watch showed that he was out of time. Swearing softly, he reached for the Glock. "Since I don't have time to argue with you, you can stay." He pressed his fingers against her lips. "Not another word. Don't move from this spot."

Her eyes gleaming with excitement, Lani nodded. A moment later, he half-turned and signaled her once again to remain where she was. Then he disappeared into the thick, tropical foliage. The only sounds were the lonely rustle of the night wind, the soft sigh of the surf, and Lani's heart as it pounded in her ears.

• • •

THE PILOT, A retired Navy SEAL now working for a private executive security company that Nick, the moonlighting cop/bartender/brewer, had hooked him up with, was as good as advertised.

As he and Donovan burst into the cabin, there was no conversation. No threats, confessions, any of that stuff that tended to fill up the last twenty minutes of a movie where the bad guys shared all that they'd been up to, and ended up getting either arrested, or, shot by the good guys, who walked away, either with the girl or each other, if it was a buddy flick.

The thugs who'd been pounding their fists into Ford Britton's face spun around, guns drawn. And wouldn't you know it, they held the guns sideways, like gangsters always did in the movies, and, as Donovan had learned on a couple of earlier occasions in his vice days, in real life. Which might allow for a quick draw and look real cool, especially up on a big screen, but was a piss-poor way to get an accurate aim.

Fortunately, because he and the SEAL had been taught the double-handed, thumb forward hold (because, dude, it helps to point in the direction you actually want the bullet to go), the rapid-fire exchange ended up good guys two, bad guys, zero. And the dumb guy tied to the chair screaming like a girl as he pissed his pants.

"I suppose you should untie him," the SEAL/pilot drawled.

"Why me?" Donovan asked, wondering how many times FBI guys ever actually used those guns he saw in the weapons vault. He was used to talking things out. He'd been trained to do exactly that. But there was a reason he spent all that time at the range. Because sometimes either the bad guys had nothing to lose or were idiots. From what he knew about the way Capelli handled family business, he suspected, for these two, it had been six of one and one-half dozen of another. Because the odds were that they'd be dead either way.

"Because it's your mission. I'm technically not here."

"Talk about a cop-out." Donovan had stuck the Glock back into his jeans when Lani suddenly showed up. And, dammit all to hell, she was not alone.

23

WHEN THE EXPLOSIVE sound of a gunshot shattered the night, Lani instinctively crouched down and wrapped her arms around herself. Another shot rang out, fading into the darkness as the night fell silent once again. The ominous quiet was unnerving.

With the gunshots still ringing in her ears, she made her way stealthily toward the shack, following Donovan's example by keeping hidden in the shadows as best she could.

She'd almost reached the open door when an arm reached out from behind a tree and grabbed her around the neck.

"One word," the man growled in her ear as he pressed a gun painfully into her side, "or if you try anything, you're a dead woman. Is that perfectly clear?"

She nodded, fighting for calm, even as her blood chilled to ice and her body trembled. As he pushed her into the one-room cabin, she saw two men lying on the floor, guns still in their hands. They weren't moving.

"Fuck," Donovan muttered.

The pilot, whose casual ease with the dangerous situation suggested piloting charter planes was not his usual occupation, said nothing. But he did roll his eyes.

Unsurprisingly, neither man appeared at all happy to see her.

Ford, or she had to assume it was him, since his once handsome face was unrecognizable, was tied, hand and foot, to a wooden chair. What little bit of blue eyes weren't buried in swollen black-and-blue bruises, were wide with fear, and he'd wet himself.

Not that she blamed him for that.

"Here's the deal," the thug who'd grabbed her told Donovan. "First off, unless you want me to shoot the little lady right now, you're both going to drop your weapons."

"Are you okay?" Donovan asked her.

"I'm fine." *Liar, liar, pants on fire.*

"I don't remember inviting chatting," her captor said. "Drop. The. Fucking. Guns. Now." She couldn't help a slight cringe as the gun pressed deeper into her side. Toward the back, which she remembered from one of the *Jeopardy!* answers was not that far from her kidney.

She gave Donovan her most sincere "I'm so sorry," look, but his face remained expressionless. As did the face of the man who was definitely no mere pilot.

Even as both men dropped their pistols as ordered, Lani felt a spark of encouragement. Ford was obviously going to be no help. The way she saw it, there were three against one. Two of whom were professionals trained to handle situations like this. The odds were in their favor.

"Now, your friend here is going to tell me where the ship's vault is."

"You're taking a big risk for not that much dough," Donovan said.

"It might be," the only man left holding a weapon agreed. "But there's also three million dollars in uncut diamonds in the vault."

"Which weren't on the manifest," Donovan said.

"Oops," her captor said. "I wonder how those got overlooked."

"Must've been some careless dockworker," Donovan suggested in a dry tone.

Lani recognized what he was doing. Keeping the bad guy talking while he came up with a plan. The only problem was, if she knew the ploy, the bad guy probably did as well. She might watch bad guys on TV, but the thug with the gun actually played one in real life.

Still, she considered, that didn't discount the element of surprise.

Fed up with the way these men were ruining Christmas and her plans for the upcoming romantic New Year's, when, as the clock struck midnight, Lani was going to tell Donovan that she loved him, she shifted her weight and took a deep breath.

Her surprised captor shouted as he slipped through the air, landing with a thud on top of one of his former gang members.

"Damn," Donovan said, as the pilot retrieved the gun from the guy on the floor, then with one well-placed punch, knocked him out. "You really do know judo."

"I told you I had a brown belt," she reminded him. "It may not be a third degree, but this guy was easy. I could've handled him back at my green-belt level."

Now that the excitement was over, a rushing sound was filling Lani's head, and her knees were suddenly turning as weak as water. As she felt the blood leaving her face, Donovan took her into his arms. "Take a deep breath," he said. "And sit down."

She glanced down at the floor that was mostly taken up with two dead and one unconscious bad guy. Which didn't make his advice the most appealing she'd ever been given.

"I'll be fine," she assured him as she shook her head to clear it, then wished she hadn't.

He'd just picked her up in his arms when three more men came tearing through the open door, guns drawn, faces grim. Would this night never end?

"You guys missed all the fun," Donovan drawled.

"We thought we'd leave that to you." A broad grin split Chief Kanualu's dark face. "Professional courtesy, along with island hospitality, and all that."

"I appreciate it," Donovan said. "How'd we do with Capelli?"

"The federal boys took him into custody as soon as his jet touched down." The police chief shook his head. "Unfortunately he didn't seem to appreciate our aloha spirit."

"I can't understand that," Donovan said with a smile of his own.

"Neither can I," Manny Kanualu agreed. "After all, it's not like we greet every haole who arrives in the islands personally."

He beamed with obvious satisfaction as he tipped his hat toward Lani. *"Mele Kalikimaka,* Lani. It's good to see you. Donovan told me you'd probably be coming along. My wife's going to write a proper thank you note, but please tell your parents how much we enjoyed this year's luau bash. The snow was inspired. Our grandkids had a super time."

• • •

"YOU HAD THE police in on this from the beginning," Lani accused Donovan as they lay in his bed, arms wrapped around each other, while the sun rose outside the window.

Donovan brushed a strand of fiery hair away from her face. "Not exactly from the beginning, but once I figured out what was going down, I thought the least I could do was share the information. I know I hate it when some other jurisdiction is messing around in my precinct without informing me ahead of time. It's also a good way to get shot.

"Besides, once those FBI guys started following us, I didn't have any choice but to fill them in before they got the wrong idea and decided we were working with Britton."

"That was nice the way you told everyone that Ford had every intention of turning the money over to the government."

Donovan shrugged as he ran his hand down her side. "Maybe he really did have that in mind all along, hoping to negotiate a finder's fee. You didn't see him arguing, did you?"

His mouth created a sizzling path along the slope of Lani's breasts, and her voice grew husky with desire as she tried to concentrate on their conversation. "Would you have argued if you'd been in his shoes?"

"Hell, no." The damp heat of his mouth moved with tantalizing slowness down her body, leaving trails of exquisite lightning.

"You lied to me, Donovan."

"And you lied to me." Sighing heavily, he reluctantly stopped his seductive kisses and lifted himself up on his forearms. "Dammit, Lani, do you have any idea how much danger you could have been in?"

She smiled up at him, framing his scowling face with her palms. "Don't be silly. I was with you."

"I think it's a toss-up," he said finally.

She pressed her lips against his. "What?"

"Which one of us is going to drive the other crazier."

Lani could feel his smile against her mouth. "You're probably right," she agreed cheerfully. "But think how much fun we'll have in the meantime."

With a groan that was part agreement, part anticipation, Donovan lowered his body onto hers, locking her securely under him with his thigh. That was the last either of them had to say for a very long time.

24

THIS WAS, LANI considered happily, as she awoke in Nate's house the next morning, a delicious way to live. She leaned over and pressed a quick kiss against Donovan's tanned cheek before getting up. Sliding out from under the sheet, taking care not to wake him, she left the house on her customary morning walk along the beach. The sharp tang of the salt air cleared her head, and the comforting swish of the warm tropical water against her ankles soothed the anxiety created by thoughts of Donovan's inevitable return to Oregon.

Fully restored to her usual good humor after what could have been a horrific night, she practically skipped up the steps and entered the house. Her smile faded when she discovered Donovan on his phone. His dark frown left her no doubt that the call was business, not pleasure.

It's the commissioner, he scrawled on a notepad beside the phone.

Lani's heart skipped a beat. It wasn't time, she thought. They still had another week until New Year's. But the frown lines that she remembered from his arrival on the island gave her the distinct feeling that this call was going to take Donovan away from her.

"I've got work to do. I'll see you later," she said.

Donovan caught her by the wrist. "Wait a minute," he said before turning his attention back to his caller. "Jack, give me just a minute, okay? Something's come up."

He covered the phone with his free hand. "I thought, now that we've gotten Britton back safe and sound, that we were going to Fern Grotto Restaurant for brunch this morning."

"We were," she agreed. "But that was before the commissioner called."

"He doesn't have anything to do with us."

Doesn't he? Lani was tempted to ask. But that would be breaking the rules she had insisted on from the beginning. No ties. No commitment. Just two people—a man and a woman—enjoying each other for as long as their time together lasted. That was all this interlude with Donovan could be. It was all she could allow it to be.

"All right. He's forgotten." She touched her fingers to her lips, then his. "I'll see you later." Lani felt as if the forced smile was about to freeze on her face.

"Later," Donovan agreed as she left the house.

As he watched her walk away down the beach, Donovan considered hanging up on the commissioner and following her, but prudence and self-discipline won out, and he reluctantly decided not to give in to the tempting impulse.

Besides, Donovan reminded himself, he and Lani had an agreement. No strings. No ties. It was without a doubt a practical, sensible rule. And he was nothing if not a practical, sensible man. Ignoring the little flicker of doubt in the back of his mind, Donovan returned his attention to the obviously harried man who'd interrupted his vacation in paradise.

Unable to keep her mind on her work, Lani paced the floor of her own house, determined not to think of Donovan. But that proved impossible as her rebellious eyes kept drifting toward the sparkling curve of coral sand, watching for him. Waiting for him.

"This is ridiculous," she muttered, glaring out over the turquoise water. "You just got carried away. You can't possibly love the man. His world is light-years away from yours."

He was also not interested in commitment or permanency, she reminded herself firmly. He'd told her that from the beginning. To expect a future where none existed was sheer folly. And that, Lani considered, was the crux of her problem.

Annoyed with herself, she sat down at her rattan desk and turned on her computer, researching topics for a student version of *Jeopardy!* the library would be putting on in the new year. After all, she strongly doubted that Donovan was over at Nate's house, fretting about their relationship. No, he was undoubtedly deeply immersed in the reason for the commissioner's telephone call, his attention focused solely on his own future. His own ambitions. Determined to do likewise, Lani began to read.

"That must be some dynamite topic."

As Donovan's deep voice broke her concentration, Lani lifted her head, surprised to see him standing over her.

"I didn't hear you come in."

"I knocked, but your mind was obviously somewhere else."

"Arizona."

"Arizona?"

"It's illegal to hunt camels in the state of Arizona," she explained.

Donovan smiled. "I'll keep that in mind the next time I visit Phoenix."

Lani nodded. "I certainly hope you will. After all, it wouldn't do for an FBI agent to be arrested for camel poaching."

"The powers that be would probably hit the roof," Donovan agreed easily as he pulled up a chair.

"And wouldn't that be a disaster," she muttered.

His brow furrowed in response to her acid tone. "Are we fighting?"

"No."

He continued to study her thoughtfully. "Good. Because I don't want to waste time fighting, Lani. Not with you. Not now." He took her hand in his.

"Are you going to tell me what that call was about?" she asked, struggling to keep her voice steady as he brushed his thumb lightly over her knuckles. How was it that such an innocent touch could make her feel as if her bones were melting?

"I can think of better things to do than to talk about the commissioner." The sexy gleam in his deep blue eyes reminded Lani that their relationship had been based on mutual pleasure.

"You're not answering my question, Donovan."

He ran his palm up her arm. "Why don't we talk about him later?"

"Why not talk about him now?"

Muttering an oath, Donovan forced his mind off the satiny texture of Lani's skin and back to their conversation. He didn't want to waste time talking. Despite his need to make love to Lani, Donovan knew that by ignoring her repeated request, he would be giving her the idea that the only thing he wanted—or needed—from her was sex.

Though the sex was admittedly the best he'd ever experienced, Donovan knew that something else was happening. Something that he'd vowed to figure out by New Year's. Unfortunately, his time had just run out.

"Martin Henderson, the current police chief, had a heart attack early this morning."

Lani drew in her breath. "Is he—"

"He's going to be all right," Donovan said. "But it forces his retirement a few weeks early. At the moment, Portland is without a chief of police, which is the reason for the call. Now can we make love?"

"In a bit of a hurry, aren't you?"

"I don't have any choice. The plane leaves from Kaua'i in less than three hours to make a connecting flight in Honolulu to the mainline."

Lani had been expecting this since the moment she had entered Nate's kitchen and seen Donovan's grim face. The news came as no real surprise. Why did she feel so miserable? She forced back the stinging tears behind her eyelids, vowing that she would not cry. She would not ruin what had been an idyllic holiday by behaving like a clinging female.

Annoyance was the safest emotion Lani was experiencing at that moment. Allowing it to surface, she struggled to keep her voice steady. "Don't let me hold you up."

"I want you to come with me, Lani."

Lani struggled to read the real message in Donovan's suddenly shuttered blue eyes. What was he asking of her? "To Portland? Why?"

"I don't like the idea of being away from you," he said. His calm tone concealed the fact that a giant hand seemed to be squeezing his gut in two. "I thought you might be feeling the same way."

Lani felt as if she were treading on eggshells and didn't particularly care for the sensation. She had always been the frankest one in the family—with the admitted exception of her grandmother—but this morning she found herself censoring not only her words but also her thoughts.

"Oh, Donovan," she said regretfully.

He frowned, wishing, not for the first time, that women came with a manual. Had he misread what they'd shared? Had those blissful hours meant so much more to him than they had to her?

Donovan didn't think so. He decided that for some inexplicable reason, Lani was still afraid to commit herself. And as much as he wanted to demand that she stay with him at least long enough to watch their grandchildren feeding frozen peas to Moby Dick's progeny, he also didn't want to push her into doing something she'd later regret.

He toyed with the ends of her hair. "You'd like Portland."

"I always have," she agreed. "How long would I be away?"

"I was hoping you'd want to move in with me. Indefinitely."

"I don't understand. I thought you were aiming for an FBI appointment."

"I was. And maybe still will, down the road. But this is an equally good opportunity. And you're the one who pointed out that I wanted to help people. Being a police chief is a good way to do that."

"I've no doubt you'll make a dandy chief," she said. "Of course you'll have to buy cases of those antacids you were popping steadily when you first arrived here, but the raise in pay should cover the increased medical bills."

"I was under a lot of stress. That's what this vacation was all about."

"And you really don't believe the stress will be worse when you get back to the city and take over the entire department?"

"It'll be rough in the beginning," he admitted. "But things will eventually calm down."

"Will they?" she asked quietly.

His fingers tightened. "Okay, so maybe they won't. But the pressure-cooker atmosphere comes with the territory, Lani. It's a package deal."

"If it's so terrible, why do you want the job at all?"

"Because it's a terrific opportunity."

"Will it make you happy?"

Her words put him on the defensive by causing him to recall the conversation he'd had with Thomas. "Dammit, I'm not your father!"

"I didn't think you were," she said mildly.

"Yet you're comparing me with him."

"No. I'm only comparing your situations. My father was a highly respected surgeon, an important man—"

"Who didn't exactly chuck it all to live out a Gauguin fantasy, Lani," Donovan pointed out. He knew he was handling this badly but couldn't seem to figure out an exit plan. "He didn't stop being a doctor."

"And there's no need for you to stop being a policeman," she insisted. "Just why do you have to be chief?"

How could she not understand? "For us!" he shouted. "Okay, sure, it's a great offer and I'm proud to have been the one chosen. But it'll be good for you. For us."

Lani could only stare at him. "But I don't want you to be a police chief, Donovan. Oh, I might feel differently if I thought it would really make you happy. But I don't believe it will."

"I suppose you'd be contented living with a mere cop?"

Lani wondered what was behind his acid tone. "Of course. If he loved me, I'd also be happy living with a beachcomber. As long as he was a happy beachcomber."

"That's easy for you to say when you live down here in Lotusland, talking to fish, reading fairy tales to kids, collecting seashells, and wishing on rainbows."

That stung. Lani rubbed her throbbing temple with trembling fingertips even as she felt a painful fissure open up in her heart. "I certainly understand how it is to be driven, Donovan," she said quietly. "Believe it or not, I used to be a workaholic myself."

"You're kidding." He would have been no more surprised if Lani had suddenly told him that she was a Soviet spy.

She took a deep breath, wanting her voice to be strong. "No, I'm not. Six years ago, I was making quite a name for myself in television."

"I know. Nate told me about your show. I watched it once. It was a lot better than I'd expected."

"Damned with faint praise," she murmured. "Believe it or not, in my world, I was nearly as important as you are in yours."

He sat down on the arm of the chair and took her hand in his. "What happened?"

"Since you saw *Beauty Tames the Beast*, you understand the concept. It wasn't like *The Bachelor* franchise, where the end result is a proposal, but if some romances came out of the season, ratings went up, so they were always encouraged. Which is why every contestant had to sign a contract that he or she wasn't in a relationship."

"Okay. That sounds reasonable."

"The only problem was, one of the Beauties had broken up with her boyfriend and auditioned for the program as a way to get past the breakup. Which probably wasn't the best idea, but hey, it wasn't my job to judge. Just to be a producer, which was essentially wrangling the contestants—"

"Sounds like herding cats."

"You're close." She liked that he got it. Maybe there was a chance for them, after all. "Anyway, a few weeks in, she realized she was pregnant. Which I'd already suspected, and when I asked her straight out, she told me the truth. But we were getting close to the end, and she was definitely an audience favorite. So both the senior producer, who, I suppose I should mention, I was sort of romantically involved with for a short time, and the owner of the show insisted I just let things play out. Which might have worked out.

"But the contestants themselves were living in a sort of Beverly Hills prison. They had their phones taken away, they didn't get to watch any TV but movie DVDs, and they were totally cut off from the real world."

"Which doesn't exactly define 'reality.'"

"Believe me, there's very little reality about the concept. While, on our show, the drama wasn't planned, it's not that difficult, after everyone's been forced together into such an environment, to play on various distrusts and paranoia. This particular woman was getting more and more stressed out because not only was she dealing with a first trimester of pregnancy, with all the morning sickness and hormone swings that entails, she couldn't even tell her former boyfriend, he was going to be a father.

"She told me privately that she wanted to give their relationship a second try. But contractually, she couldn't leave without the risk of the show suing her. My job was to keep her as steady as possible and get her to the end."

"Which didn't happen," he guessed.

"Wow. You really didn't watch much TV. Or YouTube."

"I was a bit busy tracking down a serial killer," he reminded her. "That didn't leave much time for entertainment."

"Touché," Lani said with a long sigh. "Anyway, I thought we were going to make it. Then she miscarried."

"Hell."

"That's putting it mildly. I argued that now we had to let her go home to her family. And maybe the baby's father. But the producer—"

"Who you had the sort-of thing with," he said.

"Yes. And I could add that it was *nothing* like our thing, but it's a moot point. So, moving on, that's when the show's attorneys stated that since she'd lied on her contract about how long she'd been out of any relationship, she wasn't owed anything. Her medical bills weren't even going to be paid. That was bad enough, but when I went to the hospital to try to break the news to her, I walked in the room and found a camera crew."

"Jesus."

"Different team," she corrected with a shake of her head. "That's when I lost it and blew up, and all my pent-up frustration and anger came boiling out. Unfortunately, the camera was still rolling, which risked ruining her life and any chance she might have had of reconciling with her boyfriend, who wasn't at all happy that she'd been keeping that secret to stay on a TV show, never mind that she was contractually obligated. Also, she'd told me that she'd gone on partly because she needed the money after the breakup since she'd been living in a house that her boyfriend had bought, and was suddenly in a financial bind."

"That's tough."

"Isn't it? Although the video of my tantrum was edited from the program, someone sold the outtake to one of those horrid Hollywood gossip blogging sites, and I became a viral sensation. I was even a popular Internet meme and Twitter GIF. Then fortunately, for me, at least, two weeks later, a paparazzi cameraman caught a big-name pop star naked on a beach with one of his bandmate's wives, and I became yesterday's gossip news."

"Do you know what happened to her? The contestant?"

"I do, actually. She emailed me. She married the boyfriend, and they have a nine-month-old daughter they did not name Beauty."

"So, all's well that ends well. Do you ever think that you could be happy doing something else, like working in a library, back on the mainland?"

Lani shook her head. "I belong here on Orchid Island."

"You're hiding from reality here," he insisted.

"I understand why you'd think that. And maybe I am. But I like the person I've become, Donovan. I thought you did, too."

"Of course I do, but you can be that person in Portland just as well," he insisted, almost shouting.

Lani had been considering that from the beginning. From the day she had first started falling in love with a man from the mainland. She shook her head decisively.

"No, I couldn't. If I moved there, I couldn't just sit around waiting for you to come home. Pretty soon I'd be back in my old routine of losing myself in a job, and you'd either be spending all your time trying to soothe the commissioner and wheedle money out of the city council for the police department, and there we'd be, two workaholics who'd be lucky if they saw each other for five minutes a week."

She was close to tears. "We'd destroy everything we have together, Donovan. And that would break my heart." Her eyes filled and she forced herself to look out over the sparkling turquoise water.

"But you're tossing it away by not coming with me," he argued.

She rubbed away the free-falling tears with her knuckles. "I don't have any choice."

"We're going to have to talk about this some more," he insisted. "You can't just drop all this on me out of the blue when I have a plane to catch."

"There's nothing left to say."

He reached out and cupped her downcast chin in his hand, lifting her tear-stained face to his. "We're not finished yet, Lani, not by a long shot."

As his mouth covered hers, a treacherous sob escaped her lips.

As he began walking down the beach, back to Nate's house, with plans to turn the rental in to Kenny at the ferry dock, Donovan felt his own eyes burning.

25

TWO WEEKS AFTER leaving Orchid Island, and Lani, Donovan sat in the dark, nursing a tall glass of Scotch, which had, until his trip to the island always been his drink of choice. Now he found himself wishing he'd stopped at the liquor store on the way home and picked up a bottle of rum.

The apartment building was located on the river, the scene from every window spectacular. As the purple shadows of dusk gave way to night, the moon created mysterious shadows in the mist that hung over the icy waters of the river.

The city lights were wrapped in a soft blanket of fog that dulled their brightness, and down on the darkened streets, the car lights looked like fallen stars. The magnificent view had never failed to lift his spirits. That night was an exception.

He wasn't a special agent. But he *was* chief of police. After years of climbing the ladder, the mist-draped city was his. So why did he feel so fucking rotten? The answer was simple: Lani wasn't here to share it with him.

Before the appointment had been announced that afternoon, he'd had lunch with a furious Nate. Over thick steak sandwiches, Lani's brother had accused him of being at best a damned fool. Or at worst, a bastard. Donovan had readily agreed on both counts.

"So go to her," Nate had insisted.

"And lose my job? I'm not the kind of man to let my wife support me."

Nate had muttered a pungent oath that Donovan, in years of police work, had never heard. "So you get a damned job on Orchid Island," he said. "What's so hard about that?"

"Doing what? Tending bar at The Blue Parrot?"

Nate had tossed back his head and polished off his beer. "You're supposed to be an intelligent man," he growled as he got up from the table. "You fucking figure something out." With that, he had marched out of the restaurant.

•••

LANI WAS AWARE of him the moment he entered the beach house. First there was the slight squeak of the screen door being opened, then the soft swish of her bedroom door, followed by his footsteps as he made his way toward the bed. All these sounds drifting into her subconscious mind as she slept told Lani that Donovan had returned.

But it was something far more elemental, emanating from the very essence of the man, that roused her to instant awareness. She sat up, pushing her tumbled hair out of her eyes.

"I'm so glad you're back," she whispered.

The mattress sagged as he sat on the edge of the bed. "You don't sound very surprised," he said, his lips caressing her scented hair.

Lani traced his face with her fingertips, as if to reassure herself that this was not a dream. "I wished for you. And here you are."

Nuzzling against the soft, fragrant cloud of her hair, Donovan nodded. "And here I am."

He drew her into his arms, running his hands up and down her back. The satin of her sleep shirt was cool against his palms, but Donovan knew that her skin would be warm.

He kissed her then because they had been much too long apart. Although by the calendar it had been two weeks and two days since they'd been together, since he had held her in his arms, Donovan felt as if it had been a lifetime ago.

"You didn't lock your door."

"This is Orchid Island, remember?"

"How could I forget...I've come to a decision," he said, fighting to remain calm while his stomach went on a roller coaster ride.

His lips, as they lingered at her throat, were more intoxicating than champagne. Her blood hummed under their touch.

"A decision?" Lani asked.

He reached out and turned on the bedside lamp, flooding the room with light.

"I don't believe it," she said, staring at him as a glimmer of hope made her dizzy.

"What?" Donovan demanded, feeling unreasonably nervous. He followed her gaze to his vivid aloha shirt. "Oh, this. I bought it at the airport when I got in."

His casual white cotton slacks that Lani had talked him into buying for the luau were rumpled from all those hours on the plane, his eyes were bleary and red-rimmed from lack of sleep, and he needed a shave. Lani thought he looked wonderful.

"It looks very good on you," she said.

"Think so?" Donovan had felt a little foolish buying the red-and-orange flowered shirt, but the saleswoman had assured him he looked just like a true *kamaaina*. "I have to admit it's comfortable."

"You look very sexy," Lani assured him. "Even better than Tom Selleck. Why, you'll have to fight the women off with a stick."

"I don't want any other women. I only want you, Lani." His expression suddenly became sober as he handed her a small box tied with gold cord. "I brought you a present."

"I absolutely adore presents," she said with a warm smile that reminded Donovan of a tropical sunrise.

"It isn't emeralds," he apologized uneasily. "Or diamonds or any of the expensive things you deserve."

"Donovan—"

"But," he said gruffly, "it reminded me of you."

His rough, serious tone almost proved her undoing. With fingers that trembled slightly, Lani slipped the gilt cord from the white box. She lifted the lid, giving a small sigh of pleasure at the piece of stained glass that nestled on a bed of white tissue paper.

"It's lovely. Thank you." She lifted the rainbow sun-catcher up to the light. Her walls, her ceiling, the floor were all suddenly covered with rainbows.

"There's a card."

So there was. Lani was nervous as she plucked the small card from the tissue. *There's a lifetime of rainbows out there,*

Donovan had written in his bold, precise hand. *Let's wish on them all together.*

"Oh, Donovan."

His stomach was twisted into knots as he took both her hands in his. "I know we had an agreement," he began seriously.

"That doesn't—"

He immediately cut her off with an impatient wave of his hand. "An agreement that made a great deal of sense at the time. You were happy here living on the island; you had your family, your work, your snorkeling. Horatio. Moby Dick.

"I was fighting off a case of professional burnout and planning on getting on an even faster track than the one that had killed my partner. Neither of us had the time or the inclination to get involved. It would have been highly impractical."

"Highly," Lani agreed quietly.

"Well, I don't care about practicalities any longer. I don't give a damn about what's sensible and what isn't, what's prudent or not. I know I swore I wasn't looking for a wife, but that was before I met you. Before I knew how good things could be between us. So I'm revoking that agreement here and now."

Frustrated by the clumsy way he was handling this, Donovan had to stop. Nervously, he jammed his hands into his pockets and began pacing the bedroom.

"I've been thinking about what you said. You're right, I wasn't very happy anymore as a detective and I would have been miserable as chief. I became a cop to help people, to try to make a difference. Not to spend all my time playing political football."

"When did you come to that conclusion?" she asked.

He lifted his shoulders in a weary shrug. "I don't know exactly. I suppose tracking down Britton had something to do with it. I'd been in a supervisory position for so long that I'd forgotten how much I liked to get out on the streets."

His expression was grim, unyielding. "I've resigned, Lani. And I've come back to Orchid Island because I need you."

Lani examined her nails. "Are you by any chance asking me to marry you, Donovan?"

"Of course I am."

"Oh."

This wasn't going at all the way he'd planned. Donovan wondered if Nate could write a how-to-deal-with-women manual between novels. He'd be the first customer. "Damn."

"Now that's romantic."

"I forgot the most important part."

Seeing the distress on Donovan's face, Lani took pity on him. Rising from the bed, she kissed him with all the fervor of a woman in love. When she finally tilted her head back, her eyes were sparkling.

"I'm listening."

Donovan took a deep breath. "I love you, Lani Breslin."

Joy, pure and bright, bubbled through her. "How handy Since I love you, too."

He ran the back of his hand down her cheek. "I don't want to give up investigative work."

"We have policemen on Orchid Island, too, Donovan," she reminded him.

"I know. But I don't want my life to be so regimented anymore. I want to be able to slow down. Live on island time with you. Which is why I decided to open up my own detective agency."

"Like Magnum P.I?"

"But without the Ferrari. And no short shorts. And I wouldn't expect to be living in a gated mansion anytime soon."

"I've never wanted to live in a mansion. But maybe you could wear those short shorts around home? Just for me? Because I think you'd look amazingly hot in them."

"For you...anything. There's something else."

"What's that?"

"I know you have your library work, and your handy-woman work, but I thought, just maybe, you'd like to help with research."

"You want us to be partners?"

"Only if you want to," he said.

"Quinn and Quinn Island Investigations." She said it out loud. "I love it."

"Then you'll marry me?"

"Since my entire family would disown me if I didn't," she said, "I think I'll let you talk me into it."

Her smile was dazzling, rivaling the brilliant radiance of the Orchid Island sun as it gifted the early morning sky with shafts of purest gold.

Lani held out her arms. "*Aloha nui*, Donovan. Welcome home."

THE END

To keep up with publication dates, other news, and a chance to win books and other cool stuff, subscribe to the JoAnn Ross newsletter from her website at www.JoAnnRoss.com. Also connect with her on Facebook, Twitter, and Pinterest.

Keep reading for an excerpt from *Sunset Point*, Nate and Tess's story, published in September, 2015.

1

NATE BRESLIN HAD dreamed about her again last night. As always, she appeared in the midst of a violent thunderstorm, the black crepe of her mourning clothes swirling about her slender body in the cold, harsh wind. Without a word, she emerged from the tempest, gliding ever so slowly toward him, her hand outstretched as if reaching for his touch.

A gust of wind from the storm-tossed sea ruffled her black veil, and a sudden sulfurous flash of lightning illuminated her ghostly face. In response to the overwhelming sorrow in those lovely, soulful eyes, he held out his hand, offering whatever comfort he could.

She was closer now.

In another moment, their fingertips would touch.

Then, as always, dammit, she was gone.

• • •

GIVING UP ON any more sleep for the night, Nate sat on the porch of his Shelter Bay home perched on the edge of a cliff and looked out over the waters of the Pacific Ocean.

As he drank his coffee, he reassured himself—not for the first time—that the entire dream was nothing more than a figment of his imagination. Maybe even some weird PTSD thing he'd brought back from Iraq and Afghanistan.

He had, after all, seen a shitload of death. And rather than come home and try to forget it, Nate worked out his "issues," as the Marine shrink during his separation Transition Assistance Seminar had referred to them, by delving into the dark world of the supernatural.

He'd written his first novel after surviving Fallujah, the bloodiest battle of the Iraq War. His blog, which he'd mainly started to occupy himself during downtime, was part ground truth of war, part absurdities of military life, and part creative writing. It was his short story of gigantic camel spiders being sent out to eat enemy combatants that had gotten him noticed by the *New York Times*, which had signed him to write for their "At War" blog.

The camel story, based on an exaggerated myth of an actual carnivorous arachnid, which did not eat people or camels, fortuitously happened to be read by an editor at a New York publishing house, who'd offered him his first book contract while he was still deployed. A book that went on to win a Bram Stoker award for best first novel, stellar reviews, and the rest, as they say, was history.

Ghosts, vampires, werewolves, ghouls—these were merely his fictional stock-in-trade, nothing more. It was certainly not unusual for a story idea to come to him in the middle of the night.

On the other hand—and wasn't there always another hand?—Captain Angus MacGrath, his resident ghost, had turned out to be absolute fact. When the apparition had first appeared during the renovation of his rambling seaside home, Nate had gone online and researched the house's history. A bit more digging disclosed that the captain had drowned below these same cliffs when his ship had gone down in a storm. Which was sort of weird since Nate's last book had been about a Bermuda Triangle area off this very same coast, into which a lot of ships had disappeared or been sunk. Including the one outside his window.

It had been after he'd moved in that the mystery woman had started appearing in his dreams. The logical explanation was that she was nothing more than a potential character lurking in the dark depths of his subconscious. Even as Nate assured himself that she was nothing more than an enticing product of his creative, often twisted mind, he didn't believe it.

Not when he could still see the anguish in those lovely dark eyes even when he was awake. Not when the evocative violet scent of her perfume lingered in the rose-tinged early-morning air. Not when he could vividly recall the tingling of his fingertips when their hands had come so heartbreakingly close to touching.

Not when his midnight visitor seemed so... real.

So alive.

Gazing down at the hulking metal skeleton of the capsized ship that MacGrath had been captaining when he'd drowned at sea, Nate decided that the time had come to stop dreaming of the woman and find out who the hell she was. And what she was so desperately trying to tell him.

2

THE MULTNOMAH COUNTY district attorney's office was in its usual state of chaos. The incessant clamor of phones was escalated by the hum of competing conversations. Cardboard cups, doughnut crumbs, and wrappers from fast-food takeout meals littered desktops. The atmosphere was laced with aggravation, frustration, stale coffee, and sweat.

Tess Lombardi loved it.

She'd never minded the breathless pace that her work as a deputy district attorney entailed. On the contrary, she thrived in the midst of what could only charitably be called bedlam.

The daughter of a Portland Police Bureau detective, she'd cut her teeth on the rarefied discipline of the law. When her parents had divorced a week before her tenth birthday, Mike Brown and Claudia Lombardi had agreed that it would be best if Tess remained with her father. No one concerned had ever regretted that decision.

Claudia was free to travel the world like a beautiful, jet set social butterfly, unencumbered by a growing child. While Mike, unlike so many of his divorced friends on the force, was able to keep his daughter under both his wing and his roof.

When Tess was twelve—despite the Lombardi custom that all the women maintained their family surname—she'd announced to her father that she wanted to go to court and change her last name to his. Which was when Mike Brown had assured her that he'd always love her, whatever her name. But he also wanted her to never forget that her mother's wine-growing family could trace its direct lineage to the Lombard conquest of Tuscany in the sixth century. Having arrived from Italy in the 1800s, the Willamette Valley Lombardis had become one of the first families to commercially grow grapes.

But Mike was the son of a drug dealer who'd been killed in prison and an alcoholic mother who'd often forget she'd left her infant alone at home. He'd landed in foster care before his first birthday, had been moved to a group home for wayward and homeless boys at age three, and then self-emancipated at sixteen. Appreciating the importance of roots, he'd encouraged Tess to recognize and embrace her own.

As usual, her father's instincts had been right. While she might not carry his last name, the big, outwardly tough man with the warm and soft heart had been everything a father could be. His unreserved love had provided all the nurturing and encouragement any young girl could ever need.

Tess's fondest memories were of the times she was allowed to watch him testify in court. Detective Michael Xavier Brown of the Portland Police Bureau was more than her father. He was her superhero—Superman, Batman, and the X-Men all rolled into one husky, gregarious human being. Although she'd attended law school rather than follow him into the department, Tess never entered a courtroom without thinking how she was continuing her father's life work to gain justice for those unable to achieve it for themselves.

As she returned to her office to pick up some papers after court this afternoon, however, Tess was more than a little irritated to be running behind schedule.

When she tossed her briefcase down, the woman at the neighboring desk glanced up in surprise. "I didn't expect you back. Aren't you due in Shelter Bay by five?"

"Five thirty," Tess said. "Of all days for Larry Parker to play Perry Mason, he had to pick this one. You should have seen him on defense this morning. I could not believe one man, especially one with such a limited vocabulary, could be so long-winded.

"By the time Judge Keane declared a lunch recess, we were already running forty-five minutes late. Fortunately, the judge must've had a hot date, because he cut off testimony and sent everyone home early."

It hadn't escaped anyone's notice that ever since *Portland Monthly* magazine had named Judge Gerald Keane the city's most eligible bachelor, early adjournments were happening more and more often.

"The boost to his social life appears to have shortened the court day," Alexis Montgomery agreed. "But there's also the fact that ever since he decided to run for that vacant seat on the Court of Appeals, the judge hasn't passed up an opportunity to make a speech. I read that he was talking to the Business Alliance at a cocktail mixer at the downtown Marriott this evening."

"Finally," Tess said. "A reason to be grateful for politics. If I'd had to listen to Larry another five minutes, I'd have started slamming my head onto the desk."

"If you're driving down to Shelter Bay, it can only mean that Dana White is getting cold feet about testifying."

"She's apprehensive," Tess admitted. "But I can certainly understand her feelings. What woman would want to admit to the world that she married a man who already had twenty wives scattered throughout fifteen states?"

"Well, I wouldn't worry too much about the Shelter Bay Mrs. Schiff if I were you. Fortunately, there are enough women out there who want to see the guy drawn and quartered that we shouldn't have any trouble getting a conviction. Especially with the case Donovan handed us all tied up with that pretty red ribbon."

Donovan Quinn was a detective in the Portland Police Bureau who'd tirelessly worked the bigamist case from the beginning, tracking down all the loose ends to make that pretty bow. Like all the cases he brought to the D.A.'s office, the investigation had been impeccable, making him a prosecutor's dream detective. Having dated him a few times before they'd decided to remain friends, Tess also knew him to be one of the good guys.

"I know we don't need her," Tess agreed. "But I have the feeling Dana needs us. Her self-confidence has taken a big hit, and she sounded shaky the last time I talked with her on the phone."

Alexis leaned back in her chair. "Sometimes I think you're too softhearted to be in this business, Lombardi."

"Why don't you try telling that to the much-married Melvin Schiff?" Tess countered. "One of the reporters down at the courthouse couldn't wait to show me today's *Oregonian.*"

"That bad, huh?"

"Schiff was quoted as saying that I was such an icy bitch that if any man even was willing to have sex with me, his penis would freeze off."

"Shut up. They did not write that."

"No, they put in an asterisk for the *i* in bitch and went with a *'certain part of the anatomy'* for penis, which, I suspect, is still a more polite term than he actually used."

"The guy's a real charmer."

"Isn't he? I can't figure out what all those women saw in him."

"He's a con man," Alexis said. "I suppose, looking at the big picture, we—and all those women who fell for his slimy grifter ways—ought to be grateful he isn't some sociopath who kills his wives for their insurance money. His M.O. was to do a juggling act between families for as long as he could get away with it, clean out the bank accounts, then move on."

"Leaving them alive but devastated," Tess said. "And speaking of moving on, I'd better get going. As it is, I'm probably going to have to break every speeding law on the books to get there in time."

"At least if you get stopped, you can argue your own case. Want some company?"

Tess considered the offer for a moment, then shook her head. "I don't think so. You've been working around the clock on that arson case the past three weeks. Besides, aren't you going out with Matt tonight?"

"I could cancel. It's not as if he isn't used to it."

Which was life as normal in the D.A.'s office. Tess couldn't remember the last time she'd had a date. Nor a day off, including weekends. There were even times when she thought that if her townhouse ever became a crime scene, one look at the contents of her refrigerator and cupboards would have investigators questioning whether anyone actually lived there.

"You just happen to be engaged to the man voted Portland's second sexiest bachelor," she reminded her best friend. "And we both know he only lost first place to the judge because you guys got engaged, which took him off the market. Besides, after the hours you've been putting in, you both deserve to get lucky."

Alexis grinned. "Now that you mention it, although I meant my offer to go along to Shelter Bay for moral support, that's pretty much what I was planning when I went shopping at lunch." She reached beneath her desk and pulled out a shopping bag from Portland's premiere French lingerie boutique.

"Ooh la la." Tess lifted an ebony brow. "You're pulling out the heavy weaponry."

"You bet I am. In this designer bag, I happen to have a bustier, garter belt and hand-dyed vintage stockings designed to knock Matt's socks off...along with the rest of his clothes."

"If you weren't my best friend, I'd have to hate you," Tess, whose only sex life for too long had involved batteries, complained. She was still laughing as she left the office, headed down the hall.

• • •

Watch for Sawyer Murphy's *Hot Shot* (book #2 in the Murphy Brother's *River's Bend* series) in spring, 2016.

Welcome to River's Bend—Oregon's most western town where spurs have a job to do and cowboy hats aren't a fashion accessory.

The Shelter Bay series
The Homecoming
One Summer
On Lavender Lane
Moonshell Beach
Sea Glass Winter
Castaway Cove
Christmas in Shelter Bay (Cole and Kelli's prequel
novella in *A Christmas on Main Street*)
You Again
Beyond the Sea (pre-publication title, *A Sea Change*)
Sunset Point

The Castlelough series
A Woman's Heart
Fair Haven
Legends Lake
Briarwood Cottage
Beyond the Sea

The Shelter Bay spin-off Murphy Brothers trilogy
River's Bend (Cooper's story)
Hot Shot (Sawyer's story), spring, 2016

Orchid Island series
Sun Kissed, November, 2015

About the Author

JoAnn Ross wrote her first novella—a tragic romance about two star-crossed mallard ducks—for a second grade writing assignment.

The paper earned a gold star.

And JoAnn kept writing.

She's now written around one hundred novels (she quit keeping track long ago), has been published in twenty-six countries, and is a member of the Romance Writers of America's Honor Roll of best-selling authors. Two of her titles have been excerpted in *Cosmopolitan* magazine and her books have also been published by the Doubleday, Rhapsody, Literary Guild, and Mystery Guild book clubs.

JoAnn lives with her husband and two fuzzy rescued dogs, who pretty much rule the house, in the Pacific Northwest.

Sign up to receive the latest news from JoAnn
http://joannross.com/newsletter

Visit JoAnn's Website
http://www.joannross.com

Like JoAnn on Facebook
https://www.facebook.com/JoAnnRossBooks

Follow JoAnn on Twitter
https://twitter.com/JoAnnRoss

Follow JoAnn on Pinterest
http://pinterest.com/JoAnnRossBooks